THEN AND NOW

JULIA JARRETT

CONTENTS

Dear readers,

While this is a low angst high heat romance, there are a few potential triggers I want you to be aware of. There is on page discussion of abandonment by a parent, gambling addiction, and the eventual loss of a parent.

XOXO Julia

Chapter One

Serena

"Miss Serena, look at me!"

I inwardly wince as little Rosie Duncan spins on her toes, wobbling and almost losing her balance. She's adorable, no doubt. Graceful and coordinated? Not at all.

"Lovely, Rosie, I can't wait to see you in class next week." My teacher smile is pasted on my lips as I wave at Rosie's parents while simultaneously handing out a flyer with my class schedule to another person.

"This 'downtown business open house' is such a genius idea." Ashley's familiar voice has me sagging in relief. "Finn and Pierre were thrilled to be invited, even though the winery isn't exactly downtown. He's getting tons of traffic to his booth asking about winery tours and lots of people are signing up for the new wine club." She drops a paper bag down on the table in front of me. "And here is your very late lunch — or is it dinner by this point?"

"Who the heck cares, I'm starved. You're an angel." I tear open the bag and pull out the salad from our friend Mila's café. I haven't had a chance to get my hands on any food for most of the day, so she's not wrong about the timing of this. I'll call it *lunner.*

I sit down gratefully and eat my food quickly as Ashley smiles at people walking past. I cast a gaze over the crowd, searching out people who might be interested in dance or yoga classes. The sad truth is, I'm already looped in with all the parents, so it's slim pickings for new students. It's a problem that's increasing over time as kids decide they're too old for dance or want to try other activities. Living in a small town has plenty of perks, but a small population that doesn't grow is one of the downsides for a dance studio like mine that depends on children to fill the classes.

"Excuse me, have you got any classes for really little ones? Three years old?"

I look up from my salad to see a woman I recognize from around town but certainly don't know well. Standing up, I set aside my food and give her my biggest smile. "Yes, I run a tiny tot program for two- to four-year-olds, but it's parent participation."

The woman beams. "Excellent, that sounds perfect. Thank you." Then she picks up a class schedule, and with a quick wave, she's gone.

"I wonder why she was asking; I was sure all of her kids were adults," Ashley comments.

"Yeah, I know I've seen her around, but I have no clue who she is."

"I think she's a Donnelly. She's got a bunch of sons and one daughter, if I remember right. They brought her to the winery for a tasting on her birthday. Good-looking guys, I must say," Ashley waggles her eyebrows and smirks. "A bit young for my taste, but nice to look at, that's for sure. I didn't realise any of them have kids."

That explains why I don't know her well. Women with adult children aren't exactly my target customer base. But then, like Ashley said, why was she asking about tiny tots?

"Can I just say, thank you for helping me run the booth today?" I reply with a smile. "I know the open house is good for business, but every year it gets busier and busier."

The sound of the street musician down the road filters through the chatter and laughter of the crowd as I survey the community, looking for potential new students.

"No problem. Finn and Pierre have the winery booth under control, so I'm happy to help."

"You're coming to Hastings after all of this, right?" Ashley asks, pulling her long hair up into a ponytail. She's one of a few new additions to our town, moving here permanently after falling in love with Finn McNeil, who runs the winery just outside of town.

"I think so."

My vague reply goes unnoticed by Ashley as I work to cover up the pit in my stomach that grows every time I'm near our large group of friends or someone mentions all the life changes happening to my closest friends.

Weddings. Babies. Engagements.

It's hard not to feel just a tiny bit jealous of it all, even though I'm thrilled for them. Their businesses are flourishing, their lives are full of happiness and love, and every dream they've ever had has come true.

Meanwhile, I'm pretty sure I'm on my way to becoming the next Mrs. Henderson, destined to be alone, talking to myself as I feed the birds in the town square.

This isn't the way I pictured my life turning out, that's for sure. Twenty years ago, I thought I had it all. A scholarship to a top dance school on the East Coast, two parents who loved and supported me, and a boyfriend who was my soul mate in every sense of the word.

Funny how none of that lasted.

The good stuff never really does. Not for me, at least. But I'm happy. It took a while to get to this point where I can say that and honestly mean it, but I am.

Thankfully, the late afternoon foot traffic picks up and I can't dwell on how I'm feeling left behind while my friends' lives all change for the better. I'm too busy dancing in place to the sound of the street musicians, calling out to my students as they walk by, and sharing hugs and stories. And my crazy energy pays off. I manage to fill my sign-up sheets for the free classes I'm offering next week as a trial for new students.

The distant sound of a voice I haven't heard in almost two decades has me jolting upright in shock, my eyes scanning the crowd, even though I know I won't see him. There's no reason at all for *him* to be in Dogwood Cove. But that doesn't stop my heart from thumping wildly at the sound of a similar baritone voice.

"You okay, Serena? For a minute there, it looked like you'd seen a ghost." Ashley's voice penetrates the haze in my brain.

I don't know how to respond, so I go for the easy out — denial. "Oh yeah, totally fine. Just heard someone whose voice sounded familiar. No big deal." I wave my hand to emphasize how *not* significant it is that I thought I heard the one man to ever own my heart.

Ashley's looking at me strangely, and I'm pretty sure she knows I'm downplaying things, but thankfully, she doesn't say any more.

"Okay. If you need help taking everything back to the studio, just let me know. I'll get the guys over here. But if you're okay for now, I'm going to head back to Finn."

"You bet. Thanks for the salad!" I give her my sunniest smile. The smile that convinces moms there's no need to worry about their child's dance costume that suddenly needs to be fixed two nights before a recital, and they don't have a sewing machine. Or my poor accountant who's constantly worrying about my bottom line. The one I use when I need to convince someone that everything is fine.

I've had a lot of practice using this smile lately.

Ashley walks away and I take advantage of the slowly thinning crowd to look at all the faces again, part of me desperately wanting to see that familiar strong jaw curving into a deep smile, the other part of me terrified I wasn't imagining things.

I spot the woman from earlier, over by the gazebo. She's surrounded by young men, which lines up with what Ashley said about the family. The Donnelly's. I don't know them well, the guys all being several years younger than me and my friends. But now that I see them together, I realize I do recognize them. The girl works at Mila's café, and I think one of the twin brothers works for the fire department. The other I recognize from my accountant's office.

But it's not the four young men laughing with their mother and sister that has me suddenly feeling as if the air around me is devoid of oxygen.

No. It's the tall, muscular — more than I remember, that's for sure — sexy-as-sin man wearing cargo shorts and a white T-shirt that's molded to his torso. Blonde hair, a little messy on top, but shorter than it was in high school. He's too far away for me to see, but I know there are bright green eyes underneath those sunglasses he's wearing that tell me everything.

Leo Talbot.

The one man who has haunted my dreams for years. He's the person I thought I would be with forever at one point in my life. And he's the only man I have *ever* said those three little words to.

And now he's holding a toddler in his arms, her head tucked into the crook of his neck, exactly where I used to like to snuggle into him.

A child.

The one thing we always disagreed on.

The ache I feel at seeing him after so long is all-encompassing. My bones feel like they can no longer hold me up, and I sink down into a chair, not letting my eyes leave him. I drink him in like a person lost in the desert given their first drink of water. He looks good. Strong, calm, steady, and clearly no longer mine. His head turns slightly in my direction, and I drop like a stone to the ground behind my table, my heart thumping wildly.

Why? Don't ask me.

But there's no way I'm prepared to talk to him. Not now, probably not ever. Just seeing him again feels like the worst kind of kismet. The kind where karma bites you in the ass and shows you everything you could have had if you hadn't been too terrified of it. If you weren't *still* too terrified of it. I peek around the corner, then pull my head back quickly when I realize they're still there. Voices pass by overhead as I pretend to be looking for something on the ground. It's probably not that convincing, but I do *not* want attention on me right now.

"What are you doing down there?"

My head pops up at Paige's voice. She's my best friend and unfortunately, an incredibly observant person. She also knows more about me and my past than anyone else. I reach out and grab her arm, pulling her down beside me.

"Leo's here."

Her mouth drops open and she pushes her glasses up her nose. "I assume by your attempt at subterfuge that you mean Leo from your younger years, and you are less than thrilled to see him again."

"Yes, Paige, Leo. The boy I was in love with is now a man with a kid, and he's standing over there." I point at the group, trying to be unobtrusive about it, but when I look over, they're all gone. "Well, he was."

"You're quite certain it was the same man? It has been a long time," Paige comments, and I can hear the doubt laced in her tone.

"Yeah, I'm sure. I'd never forget him."

Paige and I stand up, and I'm grateful she doesn't say anything just now. My heart and my brain are still trying to process what's going on.

This is what I appreciate about my friendship with Paige. We're complete opposites in personality, and on the surface it doesn't make sense that we'd be as close as we are. She's reserved, incredibly smart, and an introvert through and through. I'm anything but conservative, smart enough, but let's face it, my talents lie elsewhere, and I thrive off of social interactions. Where I'm loud and crazy and passionate, Paige is quiet and thoughtful. She knows when to give me space and when to push me.

A lot like Leo used to. Maybe my friendship with her isn't so strange after all... Funny how I never thought of that until now.

"If he's here for any amount of time, you'll have to talk to him eventually."

"I realize that."

Paige pushes her glasses up her nose, a frequent habit of hers. "How will you handle that?"

I lift my shoulders up and let them fall in a helpless shrug. "Dunno. I guess I'll start with hello?"

If her eyes could roll any harder, they would.

"Serena, I realize you default to humour in times of stress, but this warrants your attention. Your immediate reaction was to hide from him, and now you think you'll be able to hold a conversation?"

"No, Paige, I don't," I reply hotly. "Honestly, I have no idea what I would say to Leo. I never let myself think about seeing him again, it hurt too much."

Paige's face falls. "I didn't realize he caused you so much pain."

No, she didn't. She couldn't, seeing as I never told anyone the full story of me and Leo. Thankfully, I'm saved from having to reply by the voice of Paige's fiancé, Wyatt.

"Hey ladies. Serena, do you need help getting stuff moved inside?"

Paige walks over to Wyatt, lifting up on her toes to kiss his cheek. I've been around so many lovey-dovey couples for over a year, I should be used to this by now. But seeing Leo has reopened the empty hole in my heart that was left when I said goodbye to him.

"Thanks, I'd appreciate it." I smile at them both, forcing my thoughts of Leo away.

"Great. Faster we get you cleaned up, faster we can head to Hastings." Wyatt claps his hands together, but all I feel is unenthused. As much as I love my friends, and as much as I thrive on being around them and being out and about, right now I just want to go home.

"Actually, I think I'm gonna pass on the pub tonight," I say, hoping it comes off casually enough that no one thinks about how out of character that is for me. I'm normally the life of the party.

"Understandable. You must be quite fatigued after today, I know I am. In fact, I would happily go straight home, but Wyatt wishes to have a beer with everyone, and I agreed to accompany him." Paige squeezes my hand, and I flash her a grateful smile. She has her moments of being so in tune with me, and I love her for it.

"Yeah, I'm sorry to back out, but I'm exhausted, and I have to get to the studio early tomorrow to work on some stuff for the winter recital. And you know I don't do mornings well."

The white lie seems to satisfy Paige and Wyatt, and we make quick work of tidying up my booth and carrying things over to the studio. After waving goodbye to them, I lock up, then climb the stairs to my apartment. Living above my workplace is perfect for so many reasons, but my favourite is the 24/7 easy access to a dance space any time I need to work out some emotions.

Like tonight.

Which is why, after a quick shower and a change into a leotard and tights, I head back downstairs. I line up my favourite playlist for when I need to unwind and press play before heading to the barre. This is where I feel the most at peace with myself.

I have spent my entire life focused on dance. From taking ballet classes as a child, I went to a top-tier dance school and was hired as a professional ballerina. I always had the eventual plan of teaching once I retired. I just never expected retirement to be forced on me the way it was.

But I've come to terms with that and even managed to find a new way to love dance through teaching.

Now my studio is about to be taken away from me. If I don't get enrollment up soon, I won't be able to make the mortgage payments. As it is, I'm walking a thin line, not paying myself anything, every penny going back into the business. No one knows. Not my friends, not my mother, nobody.

Because the one thing I've learned from the many times things have gone wrong in my life is this: the worst part is the pity I inevitably see on other people's faces.

That's something I hoped would never follow me to Dogwood Cove.

Moving away from the barre, I change the music from my warmup song to something I know will let me push all of these negative emotions back into a box in my mind.

And an hour later, sweat trickling down the small of my back, I drop to the floor and lay spread eagle, breathing heavily. My mind is clear, my body is exhausted, and I know that as soon as

I peel myself up off the floor and go take another shower, I'll fall asleep easily. This peace, the quiet in my head, I only find this after dancing.

But when I eventually crawl underneath the covers of my bed, breathing in the lavender and spruce essential oils from my diffuser, one image and one name keep popping into my head.

A tall, handsome man holding an adorable little girl. A girl who isn't mine.

Leo.

Chapter Two

Leo

People who live in small towns are weird.

The good kind of weird, don't get me wrong. The kind that says hello to you when you're walking down the street, even if they don't know you. The kind that lifts a hand or even just a couple of fingers when you drive past each other. The kind that stops to welcome you to their town as if you're some long-lost prodigal son returning home.

I guess being the new deputy chief of police is sort a big deal, but it still surprises me just how different Dogwood Cove is from the city of Vancouver.

Which is exactly why I moved here. Being a cop and a single dad to a three-year-old is hard. Like, really fucking hard.

Doing it in a busy city with no family and no support system is even harder.

Battling the fear that something will happen to me while I'm on the job, just like it did to my dad? Crippling.

Because at least I still had my mom. Violet has no one except me.

"Okay, I think that's it. Anything else you need?"

Mayor Ethan Monroe and I stand up in his office, our meeting over.

"I'm good. Excited to get started tomorrow, thank you." I shake his hand, noticing the strong grip. My first impression of him was that he seemed young to be a town mayor, but I have to admit he seems to have his shit together.

"Well, we're glad to have you on board. I know Chief Bailey is looking forward to having some backup. It's not a super busy department, but there should be enough work to keep you occupied."

We walk to the door of his office before I reply, "Honestly, I'm looking forward to a slower pace. I appreciate the opportunity to find a better balance between work and family."

"I'm sorry, I didn't realize you moved here with your family. It's a great town for kids."

It's the first time we've discussed anything outside of my work responsibilities. Even during my interview, I didn't mention my daughter. A single parent working shift work in emergency services is sometimes frowned upon, and I didn't want to take the chance of being passed over for the job.

"Just my daughter, Violet. But my aunt, uncle, and cousins live here. The Donnelly's?"

"Ah yes, Claire and Dennis. Their daughter works at my sister's café. And there's a bunch of sons, too, right?"

My eyebrows raise of their own volition; Ethan notices and chuckles. "Hey, I'm the mayor. It's my job to know everyone."

"Yeah, I guess so. And you're right, my aunt's a busy lady."

"No kidding. Okay, I'll see you around, Leo. Welcome to Dogwood Cove."

As I step out the doors of city hall, right in the middle of downtown Dogwood Cove, I pause. The grassy square is scattered with people enjoying the sunshine, and the unmistakable sound of an ice cream truck is in the distance. *This was the right move.* I knew that the moment I opened the door to the house I bought, the house that instantly felt like home. And that knowledge was solidified when my Aunt Claire met Violet, and instead of Vi's usual response of crying at strangers, she actually let Aunt Claire hold her.

We needed this. We needed family. And with my mom splitting her time between the East Coast and Arizona, and Violet's biological mom who knows where, this was the best option.

I pull my phone out of my back pocket to check the texts that came in while I was talking to Ethan. I knew it was nothing serious, because Aunt Claire knows to call, not text, if it's urgent.

SAWYER: Bro, we're heading over to Westport to get some things. Need us to pick anything up?

This is what I mean. Even the simple things, like having someone offer to grab diapers from the nearest wholesale store. But I can't resist ribbing my oldest cousin.

LEO: Yeah how do you feel about buying diapers?

SAWYER: For you? Wow I didn't know you were having issues holding it in...

LEO: Ha fucking ha. For Vi. Size 4.

SAWYER: Only because she's my favourite niece-cousin

LEO: She's your only niece-cousin.

SAWYER: Do you want the diapers or not...

LEO: Thanks man.

I jog down the steps, a smile on my face. My new job starts tomorrow, we're all moved in, Aunt Claire has agreed to babysit until I find a suitable daycare, and I can finally start giving Vi the life she deserves.

I always knew I would be a cop when I grew up, but I never knew I would also be a single dad. The truth is, I was pretty set on not having kids at all. No way was I going to risk putting a child through what I went through, listening to their mother cry herself to sleep night after night. Losing my dad to a home invasion gone wrong was a nightmare. One from which we never got to wake up.

Vi may not have lost her mom to violence the way I lost my dad, but our lives are the same in that we both only have one parent trying to fill the role of two.

I can only hope I manage to be half as good at it as my mom was.

After leaving my meeting with Ethan, I find myself pushing a cart down the narrow aisles of the Stop N Shop, the one and only grocery store in Dogwood Cove. Vi's a grumpy kid without her applesauce pouches, and I'm low on coffee. I grab the essentials and head to the front to check out, my mind already thinking ahead to dinner and getting Violet to bed. Then I need to continue searching for daycares or nannies, something so that Aunt Claire isn't stuck on childcare duty forever. She raised five kids already, she doesn't need to raise my kid as well.

But thinking about the long list of things I still need to figure out now that we've moved here is a bit distracting. So much so that I don't even realize I've hit another cart until a melodic voice I never forgot the sound of says, "Oh my God, I'm so sorry!"

Memories flash through my mind, most of them happy, but enough of them laced with anger and sadness. That voice used to tell me she loved me and always would. That voice used to tell me I was the only one for her, the only person she ever wanted.

That voice also told me it was over.

I feel like I'm in a movie and there should be some uplifting music playing as the camera pans in. That's how disconnected from reality I feel when my eyes lift and meet the hazel eyes that used to look at me with so much love and understanding in them. Only now, they're filled with shock and uncertainty.

"Serena." Her name comes out on a whisper. Of all the places I imagined running into her, a grocery store in a tiny town on Vancouver Island is not it.

"Hi, Leo," she murmurs, her tongue darting out to lick her perfect heart-shaped lips. My eyes zero in on the motion. Call it habit, call it unavoidable, call it... I don't give a fuck what. She's just as beautiful now as she was when we were younger. Maybe even more so, as her body has filled out over the years, going from a lean teenage ballerina to a willowy, beautiful woman. Her hair is the same colour of golden sunshine, hanging loose and flowing down to her mid-back.

"Why are you here?" I ask, then shake my head at the dumb question. "I mean, it's a store. You're here to shop. Sorry. Why are you in Dogwood Cove?"

Serena looks down at her hands, twisting them around the handle of her cart. "Umm, I live here."

The rock that wedged itself in my throat the second I saw her drops to my stomach. "You...here?" It seems I can't stop myself from sounding like an idiot right now. I blame it on the shock of seeing her after almost twenty years.

"Yes," she answers softly. This is not the fiery woman I remember. Even at eighteen, Serena was loud, confident, and bold. Not meek and nervous. What happened to her?

My hand darts out of its own accord and tips her chin up. That was a mistake. Because that first touch of her skin sends fiery bolts through my body, waking up parts of me that have been asleep since she left. Judging by the small gasp I hear from her, she feels it, too.

"Leo, I... " she starts, then stops, stepping back. My hands drop to my sides, and I clench my fists with the effort to not touch her again, to prove to myself that she's real. "Leo, I'm sorry. I can't do this right now."

It takes only seconds for my brain to catch up with her words, but it's too late. By the time I register what she said, she's gone, her cart abandoned in the aisle, and me along with it.

She left — again.

Only this time, I'm not letting her get away.

Memories of my relationship with Serena fill my brain the entire time I'm driving home from the store, all the way until I open the front door and hear my favourite sound.

"Daddy!"

I drop everything and open my arms wide as I crouch down with a smile. Violet comes toddling in from the kitchen as fast as her chubby little legs can carry her, and straight into my embrace. Scooping her up, I blow a raspberry on her belly, earning the giggle that she only gives to me.

"Hey baby girl, how are you?"

Violet babbles away as my gaze finds my aunt standing in the doorway to the kitchen, a smile on her face.

"Hi Aunt Claire, did today go okay?"

She pushes off of the wall and walks over, her hand cupping the back of Violet's head lovingly. "Of course it did, honey. Vi's a wonderful little girl. We played in the garden, went for a walk, and baked cookies."

"Coo-tee?" Vi's eyes go wide. "Coo-tee!"

"You, little miss, have already had three cookies."

I look at my aunt gratefully. "Thank you so much for staying with her."

"Of course, Leo. You're family. We're all so thrilled you and Violet are here now. Besides, it's not like my own kids are going to give me grandchildren any time soon, so I'll get practice being a grandma with Miss Vi."

I have to laugh at that. My five cousins are all in their thirties, and yet it's true none of them are anywhere close to settling down. Then again, I'm living proof that plans don't always matter when life gets in the way.

"Oh, before I forget, remember that dance school I was telling you about? Well, it turns out the tiny tot class is at a perfect time for us. I've signed Violet up. I'll take her on the days I'm looking after her, and maybe you can take her to a few."

Dance class.

Serena.

Like a key fitting into a lock, everything slides into place. I'm willing to bet Serena is teaching at the dance school.

The question is, why? The last time I let myself check up on her was just a few years after she broke up with me. From what I could tell, she was going to a very prestigious dance school back east, and headed for stardom in the ballet world. So how did she end up teaching in a small town on the West Coast?

More importantly, can I bring myself to be in the same room with her when she dances again, even if it's only as my daughter's teacher? There's a lot of intense memories tied up between us when it comes to Serena dancing.

But for my daughter, I'll do anything.

My aunt is still talking and I tune back in just in time for her to say, "Anyway, that's all I've got to tell you. How was your meeting with Mayor Monroe?"

"Oh, ah, it was fine. Good. I start tomorrow, four days on, four days off, rotating with the other deputy. Plus the occasional evening or night shift to get familiar with the town. Are you sure you don't mind looking after Vi?"

Aunt Claire fixes me with a look. "Leo Talbot. I've told you; it is nothing but a pleasure to look after her whenever you need me." She walks back over and pats my cheek. "And we're also here to look after you. Okay? Come for dinner soon."

I smile at the woman who, until they moved away, played the role of mom when mine was incapacitated with grief. "Thanks, Aunt Claire. We will."

We say goodbye, and then it's just the two of us.

"Okay, baby girl, dinnertime. You hungry? I am." I carry Violet back into the kitchen and strap her into her seat before grabbing a few pieces of fruit to tide her over while I finish preparing her food. There's no time to think about Serena or about her teaching my daughter's dance class until Violet is in bed.

That's when I can set free these emotions and memories that are banging down the gates of my conscious mind, trying to overwhelm me.

I have to be a father first.

I can be a brokenhearted man next.

CHAPTER THREE

Serena

If it looks like a duck and quacks like a duck...it's a duck. Right?

Which means that no matter how much my heart wants to deny the truth, Leo has clearly moved on. Not only that, but despite claiming he never wanted kids — the one thing we disagreed on as teenagers — he has a daughter he obviously adores.

I thought that seeing Leo holding a little girl so closely was my breaking point. I was so wrong. The distance between us that day and the fact he didn't see me afforded my heart a tiny bit of protection. Protection that was completely shattered when I literally ran into him at the Stop N Shop. Seeing him up close, smelling that familiar scent — the cologne I gave him our second year together — that is what destroyed me.

I know my friends realize something's going on. I've passed it off as just not feeling very well, but I haven't been acting like myself the last couple of days. Not at all. I can feel my smile is more brittle, I don't want to be around lots of people, especially not couples. Not when I'm trying desperately to figure out how I'm going to survive Leo living in town.

Today is the first tiny tot dance class since the open house. I didn't sleep last night for wondering if Leo would bring his daughter, or if his aunt would, or if they would even come at all. Maybe now that he's most likely figured out that it's my dance school, Leo won't sign her up.

Maybe his *wife* won't let him sign her up.

I make my way downstairs to the studio early. Turning on the lights, opening the blinds, and setting up the music for the class is normally a routine I enjoy. It usually fills me with excitement about another day helping children discover a love of dance.

Not today.

Today I wish I really was sick so I could cancel the class and look for plane tickets far away from here. Instead, fate is against me and just as I'm twisting my long blonde hair up into a bun, the door opens. Of course, the first inside is Claire Donnelly.

"Good morning!" she says cheerfully, Leo's little girl by her side. "We are so excited for dance class, aren't we, Vi?" Claire looks down at the child and so do I. Leo's green eyes blink up at me solemnly from the beautiful face of his daughter.

Pasting on my teacher smile, I crouch down. No matter my feelings about Leo, this little girl will only ever see sunny, happy Miss Serena, the dance teacher. "Hi there, my name is Miss Serena. What's your name?"

The girl buries her head in her aunt's side.

"I'm sorry, Violet takes a while to warm up to new people," Claire says apologetically.

I straighten and turn my smile to her. "Not a problem. I'm sure we'll be friends soon."

The door opens and some more students walk in. After taking a minute to greet everyone, I head to the front of the studio and clap my hands lightly.

"Okay dancers, let's make a big circle in the middle, please, we're going to start with a song!"

Teaching two- and three-year-old kids is definitely not easy. It's more like herding cats most of the time. But damn, they sure are cute. We play with colourful scarves, sing songs, and spin around on our toes. I can't stop my eyes from finding Violet constantly. She's adorable but so shy. I notice how reluctant she is to join in, no matter how much her aunt encourages her. But then, the song that haunts parents everywhere comes on, and she lights up.

"Okay everyone, time to pretend we're all baby sharks!" I start to weave my way around the room, one hand up on my forehead for my shark fin. "Wiggle your body like you're swimming! Now we're mommy sharks! Who's going to sing with me? Doo doo doo doo doo doo!" I look over at Violet, and finally, she's smiling, even if she is still clutching Claire's hand tightly.

Before I know it, my playlist starts the song that I always end each little kid class with, and I mentally sigh in relief. I made it through, emotions intact.

I'm in the middle of cleaning up and shifting to setting up for my next class when I hear a soft voice. "Thank you, Miss Serena, Violet and I had a lot of fun, didn't we?"

I turn just in time to see Violet give me the smallest of nods.

"You are so welcome. Violet, you are a wonderful dancer. I hope to see you again at the next class."

"Oh, you will," Claire answers, giving me a warm smile. "I think this is exactly what Violet needs."

"Will her parents be bringing her or just yourself?" I ask cautiously, hoping like hell Claire doesn't know why I'm asking. Her face turns down in a frown as her gaze drops quickly to Violet and then back to me.

"It'll mostly be me. Vi just moved here with her dad; he's the new deputy police chief, so he'll be working a lot. But I know he wants to come whenever he can." She looks down indulgently at the little girl, squeezing her hand.

He did it. Leo did it.

Hearing his aunt say he's the new deputy police chief fills me with pride. His dream of following in his father's footsteps came true, and even though I am so happy for him, I'm also incredibly sad that I wasn't there to see him achieve his goals. But it's strange Claire didn't mention the little girl's mom.

"Well, it's wonderful that you can bring her," I say brightly. "I'll see you next week."

We wave goodbye, and when the studio is finally empty, I let my head fall forward with a loud sigh. I've got twelve preschoolers arriving any minute, so any emotional break down will have to wait until later.

But later, when I push open the door to Camille's, the café Mila opened in honour of her mom, any hope I had of grabbing lunch and going next door to Paige's bookstore, which funny enough is called Pages, to freak out with my best friend is over-shadowed by what I find.

My eyes greedily drink in the sight of Leo in uniform. I never got to see this, him living his career dream of being a cop. He fills it out perfectly, and since he hasn't noticed me, I take my time, my gaze traveling over broad shoulders that fill out the crisp blue shirt of his uniform, down the tapered line of his back to that ass. Damn. He still has his baseball butt. Leo played all through high school, and it's true what they say — ball players have the best butts.

Suddenly, he turns, and my eyes flash up to meet his. Crap, he caught me ogling, evident by the tiniest smirk he's wearing.

"We keep running into each other." His voice is low, smooth, and still does something to my insides despite all the time be-tween us.

"It's a small town. Bound to happen," I reply, the words coming out all breathless and weird sounding. I clear my throat and straighten my spine. I can't run away again, not like I did the other night at the store. No, it's time to default to my usual mode. Facing problems head on. "I just finished teaching your daughter's dance class."

The play of emotions across his face is fascinating. I see every-thing from love, to concern, to guilt.

"I wondered if it was you teaching. What happened to be-coming a professional dancer?"

The familiar pang of sadness at the loss of my dance career hits me. Of course, Leo doesn't know how my life fell apart for the second time. Adopting an unaffected tone, I give the explanation that, over the years, I've found leads to the least amount of pity and questions.

"I was with the Winnipeg Ballet for a couple of years after fin-ishing up my degree. But a wrong landing led to ankle surgery, which kind of ended my career unless I wanted to go from soloist to corps de ballet. So, yeah, here I am teaching instead."

His eyes, those deep green eyes that used to look at me with nothing but adoration, melt into pity. God, I hate that.

"I'm sorry, Serena. That fucking sucks."

I lift one shoulder and try to pass it off as anything but the life-altering injury that it was. But his sympathy is genuine and touching. "No big deal, I'm happy now." Emphasis on the *now*...but he doesn't need to know that.

Leo shoves his free hand in his pocket, the other still holding the bag that I'm guessing contains his lunch. Funny how life is still carrying on around us, and no one knows that my heart is bleeding inside of my chest right now.

"I know you, Serena, and I know you must have been devas-tated. Dance was your life. You don't need to minimize things with me."

Yes, I do. Because you used to know me, but you don't anymore. You moved on.

"Seriously, I'm fine now," I say firmly.

Leo stares at me for a minute before letting his eyes fall away. "Okay. Well, I'm glad you're happy. How did you end up in Dogwood Cove?"

"A former dance colleague's mother wanted to sell her studio, and I took her up on it." I answer succinctly. "And you?" I tilt my chin up defiantly. "You've got a kid now." I can hear the accusation in my tone, and I hate it. I hate that I'm feeling petty and jealous of the fact that clearly, when Leo said he didn't want kids, he meant he didn't want kids with me.

But he doesn't rise to the bait. Instead, Leo simply nods.

Twisting the knife in my chest a little bit deeper, I follow up with, "Where's her mom?"

Better to know now than have it be a surprise in the future when some woman shows up claiming to be the love of his life.

His brows knit together. "Not in the picture."

Before I can poke and pry even further at that cryptic statement, Leo pulls out his phone. "Look, I've got to go. Staff meeting with the chief and a few others in ten minutes, and I still need to eat."

I step back, suddenly feeling beyond awkward at the arctic air between us. "Yes. Of course. Sorry. It was nice seeing you." *It was nice seeing you? No, it wasn't, it was painful and horrible.*

Leo looks at me, and when I force my eyes to meet his, I see a small glimmer of the boy I used to love. "It really was. And I guess, small town and all, I'll be seeing more of you."

He taps his phone against his leg, gives me a small, enigmatic smile, and then he's gone.

"Oh crap, did he leave? He forgot the dressing for his salad." One of the waitresses at Camille's comes rushing up to the door before turning back to me. "Hey, Serena, right? You seemed like you knew my cousin, any chance you could run this over to the police station for him?"

My eyes dart down to the name tag on her uniform. *Kat.* She must be the Donnelly sister. After all this time living here, how did I not know they were Leo's cousins?

"Umm, sorry, I can't. I've got to run, actually. I have another class to teach."

Kat shrugs. "Oh well, his problem, I guess. He'll come back if he needs it, or he'll just text me and bitch later. I assume you want your order to go?"

"Yeah, thanks."

As soon as I have my lunch, I rush back to the studio. Ranting to Paige about how insane I'm feeling will have to wait. I need to eat, answer some emails, including one from my accountant that I *really* don't want to read, and then get ready for an afternoon at the high school, working with their dance team.

Freaking out will just have to wait.

By the time I get home, I'm exhausted. Physically, because teaching four classes of dance and leading a group of teens in a dance routine would take a lot out of anyone. Mentally, because the strength it took to not obsess about Leo all day was absurd.

I pour a glass of wine and grab the bag of popcorn I always keep in my pantry. I'm pulling an Olivia Pope dinner tonight. I drop down on my couch and turn on the TV to some mindless cooking show.

It's only after my wine glass is half empty that I let myself unravel the tangle of thoughts and emotions swirling in my head after the day I've had.

The mystery of Violet's mother remains, well, a mystery, but at least I don't have to try and deal with seeing him happily in love with another woman. I've adjusted surprisingly well, if I do say so myself, to the fact that my former high school boyfriend and the closest thing to a soul mate I have ever had is suddenly living in my small town. I mean, there are coincidences, and there are *coincidences*. But I've accepted that he's here.

Which begs the next question. What do I want to do about it? If the weird energy between us today was any indication, we've got some unfinished business between us. And I know the blame for that lies completely on me. I ended things so abruptly and never explained to him the real reason why. Mostly because it took many years of therapy to figure out what that reason even was.

A fear of abandonment brought on by the sudden and unexpected divorce of my parents. That's what my therapist called it.

Your dad leaves, and after a few months of awkward phone calls, you stop hearing from him except for the odd Christmas card that gets through mail forwarding. Your mom refuses to talk about any of it and throws herself head first into "redefining herself."

That's more than enough to mess up someone's perspective on love and long-term relationships. And in my case, it was enough to make me absolutely certain that Leo and I would never survive the long distance that would separate us when we both went to university. Which is why, in my infinite teenage wisdom, I figured it would hurt less if I ended it early before letting our love disintegrate into dust.

But he doesn't know any of this. And as the slightly more rational adult that I am now, I guess I can see why he deserves to know.

The jarring sound of my phone ringing snaps me out of my sad trip down memory lane. Until, that is, I look at the caller ID. Sometimes I swear, my mother has ESP. How else would she know I was just thinking about how her divorce spiraled me into the hardest decision of my life?

"Hi Mom."

"Serena, honey. How are you? How's the studio?"

I settle back on the couch and take a sip of wine. Mom and I have one of those relationships that's perfectly fine as long as we keep our contact limited. She's come out here a few times, and we try to talk once every week or so.

We were closer when I was younger, but after my dad left, she kind of disappeared as well. Not physically but emotionally. And that disconnect has never really gone away.

"It's fine, I started a new round of classes today."

Keep the conversation light and easy. That's the key with us. We don't bother getting deep or emotional with each other anymore; we haven't since I was a teenager. The last real conversation we had, we were in a therapist's office, and I was trying to get her to explain why she and my dad hid their problems from me. She shut down and refused to say a word. That was the last time I ever bothered trying to talk to her about anything important.

"Great. Listen, I need to talk to you about something."

Her tone makes me sit up straight. This doesn't sound light and easy. Not at all.

"Okay, what's up?"

"I heard from your dad the other day."

"Wh-what?" I splutter, putting down my wine glass in shock.

"He wants to talk to you."

"No. No way! It's been years, Mom. I don't want to talk to him."

"Serena —"

"No," I cut her off. Because there is absolutely no freaking way I can handle this today. "Mom, I have to go. I'll talk to you later."

I hang up before she can say anything else and turn my phone off.

What are the chances... Leo and my father, both surfacing from my past within the last few days. I'd really love to know why the universe is deciding to dump all my emotional baggage, that I thought was dead and buried, out in the open now. *All. At. Once.*

CHAPTER FOUR

Leo

"Vi, kiddo, come on. You're covered in spaghetti. It's bath time."

"No Daddy. No baf!" Violet streaks past me, naked except for the tomato sauce covering her face and chest. These are the moments that test my patience. When it's nearing her bedtime, and I just want some peace and quiet for a couple of hours before I collapse into bed, I wish she wasn't such a stubborn toddler.

Single parenting is beyond difficult. Like, more than I ever gave my mom credit. Granted, I was a little bit older when Dad died, but still. I have a lot more understanding for what she went through, all the time battling the grief of losing her partner. Fishing out my phone, I open my text conversation with her.

LEO: Hey Mom, thinking of you. Hope Arizona's treating you well, you'll have to come up here soon. This town is beautiful.

It's a deliberate choice not to mention Serena just yet. My mom loved her, and until I know what's going on with everything there, I don't need my nosy matchmaking mother getting involved.

MOM: Hi honey, Phoenix is great. Hot! Almost too hot to be honest. I'm going to talk to Aunt Claire and figure out a trip soon, I miss my little Vi. Give her a smooch from Nana.

LEO: Will do. Love you.

I put the phone back in my pocket, shaking my head at Violet's off-key singing coming from her bedroom.

I guess the silver lining in my situation is that I definitely don't grieve Violet's mom leaving. I wish she hadn't done that to our daughter, but at the same time, it's not like Alexa was a great mom even when she was around those first few months.

Doing right by my kid is my number one goal. It has been since the day she was born, and they put this screaming, red-faced, covered in a strange baby goo newborn into my arms. I knew then and there that, no matter my reservations, she had to be my priority. Everything I've done since has been because it's what I hope is the best for her.

But it's scary as fuck making all those decisions on my own.

"Violet Talbot, get your booty in the tub right now, or you only get one bedtime story."

I hear her feet stop. If there's one thing Violet loves almost more than anything, it's her bedtime stories.

I reach the bathroom where she's standing beside the tub. "Good job, waiting for daddy. Okay, let's get you cleaned up, kiddo."

One hour, three stories, and two songs later, Violet's asleep, curled around her favourite unicorn stuffy. I stop at her doorway and watch her sleep, the same way I have every night I've been home since she was a newborn. The love I have for that child is deep and profound. It transcends reason and logic, and for the longest time I didn't think I would ever feel that way for anyone else.

I had forgotten, or maybe was in denial, about the fact that I have felt something similar before. For a particular blonde dancer who, out of nowhere, has reappeared in my life.

Knowing the mess that awaits me in the rest of the house, courtesy of hurricane Violet, I push off the wall and close her bedroom door softly. Making my way to the kitchen, I grab a beer from the fridge, turn on some music, and start cleaning up.

Just as I turn the dishwasher on, ready to tackle the living room that is covered in toys, my phone vibrates. I grab it off the table to see an unfamiliar number has sent a message.

UNKNOWN: Leo, hi. It's Serena. This is awkward, I got your number from Violet's registration form for dance class. I was hoping we could talk.

I stare down at my phone for a beat. A hundred things are running through my head. Do I want to talk to Serena? Obviously, yes. But to what end? Closure? No, because I don't want to close the door on us. Fuck, I want to tear the door off its hinges and find my way back to her.

But I've got Violet now. And she needs a father who's present and dedicated to her, not chasing some memory of a love that might not even be reciprocated anymore.

Still, I need to see her. I quickly add her info to my contacts before responding.

LEO: Hey. I'm glad you reached out. Can we get coffee tomorrow?

SERENA: Sure. I'm free in the morning, no classes til after school gets out. Meet at The Nutty Muffin?

LEO: Okay. I can probably take a break around 10.

SERENA: See you then.

I drop the phone on the table and lean against the back of one of the chairs, letting out a heavy breath. I've got fourteen hours, give or take, to figure out what to say to the woman who broke my heart.

Pushing open the door to The Nutty Muffin the next morning, my senses are assaulted in the best possible way. The distinct aroma of fresh coffee mingles with a tantalizing smell, fruity and cinnamony, and just fucking amazing. My mouth instantly starts to salivate. Serena isn't here yet, from what I can see, so I make my way to the counter to order for the two of us. Hopefully, she still drinks peppermint tea in the mornings.

A brunette greets me and she's familiar somehow, but I have no clue why.

"Hi there, Deputy Talbot, welcome to The Nutty Muffin. What can I get you?"

It takes me a second to adjust to being called by name like that; it doesn't happen very often in the city.

"Hey, I'll take a coffee with cream, a peppermint tea, and two of whatever it is that smells so good."

Her eyebrows raise as she smiles widely. "That would be the apple nut muffins." She turns and busies herself starting the drinks, then opens the glass case and pulls out two huge muffins, placing them on a plate. "Here you go. I'll bring the drinks over if you're staying, if not, just give me a second."

I turn around and spy an open table. "I'll sit over there, thanks."

Taking the muffins, I make my way over and sit down, eyes trained on the door for Serena.

"Here you go, I assume you're waiting for someone?" The nosy brunette is back, drinks in hand.

"Yeah. An old friend."

"Oh! Maybe I know them. I'm Mila Monroe, my partner is the vet, and my brother is the mayor. I've lived here my whole life, and I own this place. Safe to say, I know just about everyone."

Well, that explains why she's familiar. She does look a little bit like her brother.

"I'd say it's safe to say you know me." Serena's voice cuts in as she slides into the seat across from me. "Thanks Mila, we're good."

Mila's head swivels back and forth between Serena and me so many times it's almost comical. I press my lips together, watching Serena scowl up at the woman who I assume is a friend of hers.

"Mila. You've got customers," she says pointedly.

"Uh huh," Mila replies, then points her finger between us. "But this is far more interesting. We'll talk later, lady. Deputy, nice to meet you."

As soon as she's gone, Serena lets out a quiet groan. "I'm sorry about her. She means well, but nosy doesn't begin to cover it."

"I kind of got that sense," I say, fighting back a grin. "It's fine, Tippy."

The nickname slips out before I can catch it and we both freeze instantly.

"Wow. I haven't heard that in a long time," she whispers.

"Yeah," I croak, "I haven't exactly called anyone else Tippy Toes in a long time, either."

What started as a way for me to tease Serena about dancing en pointe turned into something special between just the two of us. My favourite was calling her Tippy when we would make love. She'd get this fierce look on her face, but secretly, I knew she adored it. And she always came really fucking hard.

"I hope you still drink peppermint tea," I say awkwardly, sliding the cup over to her. "And these muffins smelled too good to pass up."

"I do, thank you, and they're delicious. Good choice," Serena replies, and I swear she's just a little bit impressed that I still remember her favourite drink.

She blows across the steaming surface of her cup before lifting her eyes to meet mine. "Leo, I feel like I owe you an explanation." Her voice falters at the end and I impulsively cover her hand with my own.

The instant I feel her satin skin against the pads of my much rougher palms, I'm transported back in time.

The first time I held her hand, we were sixteen. It was our first date at the movie theater. I was terrified, but also hopelessly infatuated with her. She made the first move, placing her arm on the armrest between us, her palm facing up. She wiggled her fingers expectantly, and after I wiped my palm on my pants, I placed it on hers. That first contact was electric. No, it was addictive. I knew then and there, I would never want to stop holding her hand.

That feeling hasn't changed, and judging by the way her eyes are staring down at our hands, and the ever so slight rub of her thumb across my knuckles, she's feeling it, too. The wash of memories, mixed with the tantalizing temptation of possibility.

I never stopped missing Serena. I still miss the feel of her body against mine, her lips on my lips. Even the pain that's lingered for two decades inside of me doesn't change the fact that I'd give anything to feel her again.

"You don't owe me anything. We were kids, shit happens." That's not even the tiniest bit true, we may have been young, but there was nothing flippant about how I felt about her. But I've always needed to do whatever it takes to make Serena feel okay. That's why I didn't fight her when she broke up with me because I could tell, instinctively, that she needed to do it.

And taking care of her was always my first priority.

"Please, I want to at least... Oh God, I don't know." Her chin drops down to her chest, elongating the beautiful line of her neck. My fingers ache with wanting to stroke the soft skin there. But I can't. She's not mine anymore. Instead, I settle for squeezing her hand gently, internally cheering when she squeezes it back.

There's no denying I still have it bad for Serena.

"Serena, we were in love. But we were young. Whatever happened to make you feel like you needed to break it off, it's okay, I forgive you. I've never been mad at you or held it against you."

Her eyes lift to meet mine, and I can see the hesitation, the nerves, the worry layered in them.

"You know you can tell me anything, Tippy. That hasn't changed."

I can tell the second she decides to trust me on that. Her chest lifts in a deep breath, and she expels it slowly.

"My parents got divorced and my dad abandoned me."

Wow. That's not at all what I was expecting. The Mathesons always seemed so happy, the perfect united front, always there to support Serena. I imagined me and her being like them someday. Then there's the fact that I had no clue. Granted, I took off from of our hometown pretty fucking quick after Serena broke it off with me. I couldn't stand to be around all of our memories. But still, my mom never mentioned a thing.

"Wait, what? What happened?"

She lets out a harsh laugh. "I wish I knew. But their breakup messed me up. I was blindsided and I didn't handle it well. I mean, if divorce could happen to my parents, of all people, it could happen to anyone. I spent seventeen and a half years thinking I had the perfect family, two parents who loved each other, the role models of a healthy marriage, only to find out it was all a giant fucking lie."

She pulls her hand away, and I instantly miss the connection, especially given that I can feel the anger and hurt rolling off her in waves. I want to comfort her, but I can't.

"Anyway, I started to panic that you and me, what we had, was too good to be true."

She trails off, and I finish for her, "So you ended it."

Serena nods, and when she looks up at me, her eyes are glistening with unshed tears. "I did. And I'm so sorry."

We're both quiet for a moment, sipping our drinks, processing it all. I know it's on me to respond, to move us forward somehow.

"We're okay, Tippy. I'm okay. Was I sad back then? Of course. You had my heart, and you gave it back to me in tatters. But I'm fine now. You needed to make the choice that was right for you at the time, and I respected that then, and I respect it now." A tear spills down her cheek, and my thumb lifts up to swipe it away. "Don't beat yourself up any longer over what happened in the past, okay? We're good. We can move on from this, as adults."

"God, you've always known just what to say," she chokes out, leaning her cheek into my hand. "Thank you, Leo. When I did it, when I broke up with you, a part of me wished you would come after me and try to convince me not to end it. But I was also so scared that even if you did, it would end eventually, no matter what. And, you know me, I always was impatient. Couldn't stand for things to be long and drawn out."

"You also hated surprises," I say gently. "I'm guessing part of the reason you ended it was so that it wouldn't come as a surprise. You wanted control over it."

Her eyes widen. "Y-yeah. I guess so. Wow, you really did know me better than I knew myself, didn't you?"

I let my hand fall down to cup my coffee cup as I quirk my lips at her. "Yeah, I did. Which is why I'm also guessing the surprise at seeing me again hasn't been easy for you."

She gives me a watery smile in return. "No, it wasn't easy at first. But now... "

"Daddy!"

The sound of Violet's voice interrupts us at the exact wrong moment. Shit, I wonder what Serena was going to say. But the bubble we were in pops and sounds of other conversations come back to me. I twist in my seat just in time to see my aunt and Vi walking toward us. Aunt Claire has a questioning expression on her face when she sees Serena with me, but she doesn't say anything, just places Violet, who's straining to get to me, down into my lap.

"Hey, baby girl. What are you and Aunt Claire doing?"

"Muffin, pwease?" she asks, patting my cheek. I smile down at the center of my entire world, even as part of me tingles with the awareness that Serena is right there, watching.

"You bet, kiddo. Want to try Daddy's, or do you want your own?"

"Mine, pwease."

"I'll get one, Violet," Aunt Claire chimes in. "Nice to see you, Miss Serena. I didn't realize you knew my nephew." There's no malice in her tone, but plenty of curiosity, and I know I'm going to have a lot to explain later.

"Serena and I knew each other in high school," I supply, and Serena shoots me a grateful smile. Just then, Violet scrambles down out of my lap. I go to reach for her, but instead I'm stunned to watch my shy child, who doesn't take to new people easily at all, reach for Serena's sleeve.

"Dance pwetty?" she says and my mouth falls open.

Serena smiles down at Violet. "Hi sweet girl, you certainly do dance very pretty."

Vi shakes her head. "No. No Vi dance. You dance pwetty."

Serena looks up at me, biting her lip. I shrug in response. "She's right, Tippy, you do dance pretty."

What happens next does something to me. What exactly? I don't know. Serena gets out of her chair, and there in the middle of the café, she sits down on the floor and holds her hands out to Violet.

"Come on, Vi, let's show Daddy how *you* dance." Then she holds Violet's hand and helps my baby girl spin around on her toes. When she's done, Serena claps lightly, and Violet smiles brightly as she claps along with her. "That was wonderful! You're a beautiful ballerina," Serena praises as my daughter turns and walks back over to me.

"Well done, baby girl. You're amazing," I murmur into the top of her head as she snuggles in under my chin. My eyes find Serena's, and even though I know she has no clue the significance of what just happened, I mouth the words "thank you."

Because what she just did, connecting with my little girl so easily, is something no other woman has been able to do ever since Violet's mother walked out on us.

And right now, I'm having a hard time denying the idea that fate might have brought me to Dogwood Cove for more reasons than just my family and my career.

Chapter Five

Serena

Talking to Leo, even just for a short while, was apparently what I needed to snap out of the bizarre funk I've been in ever since I first saw him.

Don't get me wrong, I'm still completely confused over what to do about him being in town, but I have managed to find a tiny bit of peace with him being here. I never realized how much I needed his understanding, his forgiveness. But now that I know he doesn't hold it against me, I feel strong again.

Which is why, here at Summer and Ethan's house for book club, I'm ready. Ready to face the barrage of questions that I know are coming.

"Ladies, the party can start now. I'm here," I announce, kicking the door closed behind me before toeing off my shoes and heading into the kitchen. I am determined to be my usual self tonight, enjoy my time with my friends, and *not* obsess about Leo.

Placing the two bottles of wine I brought on the counter, I grab the already open one and pour a healthy glass before turning to face the wall of curious faces staring at me from the living room. Summer, Mila, Ashley, Paige, and Abby are all watching me closely. Too closely.

So much for not obsessing.

"Okay, okay, let's get this out of the way. His name is Leo, he's my high school boyfriend, and he just moved to town to be the new deputy chief. That's it, that's all, end of story. Any questions?"

I regret those last two words the instant Mila and Ashley's hands shoot up in the air.

"Things were looking pretty cozy between you and that little girl. Is she his daughter?" Mila asks with a cute little smile. And I won't even deny it, my heart melts a bit at the thought of Violet.

"Yes. She's adorable but shy, so do *not* overwhelm her," I stare pointedly at Mila. "And since I know what your next question will be, her mom is not around, and no, I don't know why."

Ashley is still impatiently wiggling her hand up high in the air, so I take a deep breath and turn to her next. "Yes?"

"Do you still have feelings for him?"

My heart thumps over in my chest. Do I? I mean, I can't ignore the fact that's he hotter than I remember or that I desperately want to know if he still kisses as good as he used to. But do those count as feelings or just lust?

"That's complicated. And it's going to take a lot more wine and a lot more time for me to be able to figure it out, so can I get back to you on that?"

Ashley pouts but nods. "Fine. But next book club, we expect more details."

Paige stands up and I breathe a sigh of relief. She's the voice of reason in our group, and she's also the one who's determined to try and keep us on track with the actual discussion for the book we read.

"If we are quite finished discussing Serena's former flame, could we please bring our attention to our read for this month?"

I pull my copy of *Bred For Them* out of my bag, for once eager to get to the book talk and away from me. For all that I'm a performer, this is one time I'd rather not have the limelight. And seeing as this book was, by far, the hottest one we've ever read, it should be easy to divert the topic.

"I gotta say, I was skeptical when you said this was a threesome, but goddamnit, those guys are hot together. The way they take care of Hailey is just, wow." I make a chef's kiss gesture with my hand.

The girls all make noises of agreement. If there's one thing I've learned from this book club adventure, it's that we're all a lot more dirty minded than we thought. But the books have brought us even closer, and these nights tend to be when we can share anything and everything with each other. Even though I don't really want to talk about my crazy stuff right now, I know these women are my safe place.

"No kidding. I swear when Hailey first hooked up with Bob-by, and Jameson was watching, I had to find Jackson as soon as the scene was over. If you know what I mean," Mila says with an exaggerated wink.

"Yeah, you know I grabbed my vibrator after that one," I chime in. "Two orgasms later, I was able to keep reading."

No partner, no problem when it comes to my sex life. Hell, half the time I think I do a better job than a guy would anyway. Nonetheless, it's a lonely place being the only single one left in our group. It's why I tend to tune out the ooey gooey relation-ship talk when it starts. But thankfully, the guy-on-guy action in tonight's book keeps things moving at a spicy pace when it comes to our conversation.

Later on, when we're finally cleaning everything up, I find myself lingering even as the others start to leave. When she isn't running the beach front resort her dad left her, Summer teaches a few yoga classes at my studio, and there's something I need to talk to her about but haven't had the chance.

"How are things going at the resort?" I ask as I dry one of the wineglasses we used tonight.

"Great." Summer gives me a warm smile. She's got such a calm and steady energy; I can feel it filling me in turn. "Now that I've hired Stephanie to help out, I'm not running around quite as crazily. I think she'll be a huge asset moving forward."

Here's my opening. I need Summer on board with teaching more classes because the demand for her yoga instruction is growing. Unlike the demand for my children's dance classes.

I'm terrified that I'm maxed out both on my time for classes and on potential students. But if I don't figure something out, I soon won't make my mortgage payments.

"Your waitlist for yoga is still pretty long, isn't it?"

"It is." Summer frowns slightly. "I've been thinking about how to reconfigure my class layout in the studio to accommodate more, but I don't think I can without compromising people's personal space."

"Would you teach another class?" I blurt out before I can stop and think about it.

Summer's eyes widen, but she's smiling, so hopefully, that's a good thing.

"I would love to, but I wasn't sure if you had any available time for me."

"Oh my God." I let out a huge breath. "I have time. I can make time for as many classes as you're willing to teach."

"Is everything okay?"

My teeth gnaw on my lower lip. Do I tell her?

"The truth is, I need to fill some more classes. And there's not a ton of kids in town that aren't already students. But there are plenty of adults."

"So why don't you teach the adults?"

I visibly shudder. "That is my last resort. Like, absolute last." Although, if I don't come up with another solution I may have to, even though teaching adults is my idea of torture. They're either so self-conscious that they don't relax and let their body do what it wants to do, or they think way too highly of themselves and don't take instruction very well. Either way, as a teacher, it's not my idea of fun.

Summer giggles. "You're ridiculous. But I'm happy to help you avoid your nightmare. Why don't we add two extra classes a week? I can do one more morning flow and an evening yin, if that works. Those seem to be the most popular."

My shoulders sag in relief. "That would be incredible. Thank you, I'll start contacting the waitlist tomorrow."

That's one step in the right direction. I only need, like, a thousand more and I'll be fine.

I'm in the middle of dancing freestyle to a playlist of classical music when a knock at the studio's front door startles me out of position. It's late, so the blinds on the large front windows are all down, making it impossible to see who it is. Cautiously, I lift the corner of the blind and see a cop car parked out front. Going to the front door, I call through it, "Who is it?"

"It's Leo."

There's a fluttery sensation in my stomach at his rumbling voice and I cover it with my hands. Breathing deeply, I turn the lock and take off the chain, letting him in.

He steps over the threshold, big and looming in his uniform. "Hey, sorry if I freaked you out. I'm on a night patrol and saw the lights on. Thought I'd check in on you, that's all." He runs his hand through his hair, and the obvious nervous gesture makes me melt a little inside.

"Thanks. I was just messing around." I turn and head back into the studio space and shut off my music. I can feel his eyes on me as I walk across the floor, and unbidden, my hips sway just a little bit more. When we were younger, Leo would tease me about having a sexy walk. I could see it written on his face.

I wonder if I'll see it when I turn around.

"What are you doing on patrol? I thought you were here to be some bigshot assistant something or other?" I ask, turning slowly in place. Yup. There's the look, and that fluttering in my stomach starts to heat up and spread slowly through my limbs, turning into something other than anticipation. We're alone for the first time in twenty years.

Leo chuckles. "Yeah, deputy chief. But they figured since I'm new in town, it would be a good idea to pull a few shifts on the beat just to make sure I know the lay of the land."

My eyes roll up. "Right, because Dogwood Cove is such a hotbed of crime."

Leo's gaze turns serious. "You can never be too careful, Tippy, no matter where you live."

"Okay, officer safety," I say, my tone mildly mocking.

Leo stalks over to me. "Serena, don't joke about it. I need to know you're safe."

My brows pull together over his serious tone. "Leo, is there something going on?"

His shoulders drop. "No. No. I guess it's just hard for me to shake the city cop mentality. Sorry."

On impulse, I reach over and take his hand. "Hey, don't apologize. I know you're just trying to look out for me."

We exchange a look, one loaded with history. I know Leo's story, why he became a cop in the first place. It's the same thing that caused our one and only serious disagreement when we were younger; the debate about having kids when we were older.

I know that he's always been worried about something happening to someone he cares about. And I know that his biggest fear was something happening to him and leaving behind me and his mom. It was the subject of a lot of conversations that were probably way too heavy for a couple of teenagers. But he needed to know I supported his dream, no matter the risk, no matter the sacrifice. I would have given up my desire for a family if it meant he got his dream of being a police officer.

His hand gently squeezes mine as he lifts it up slightly, his thumb running over my knuckles. "I wanted to thank you for what you're doing with Violet."

The abrupt change in subject jars me. "What are you talking about?"

"The way you got down on the floor yesterday and talked to her made her feel so happy. She hasn't connected with someone so quickly, well, ever. And since her mom took off, she's been even more withdrawn."

The raw pain behind his words hits me right in the heart. But without knowing if that pain is because of Violet, or Violet's mom, I tread carefully.

"She's an adorable kid, Leo. I'm sure you're doing great."

Slowly, he threads our fingers together. "Thanks. I'm just hoping moving here was the right choice. Having my family around is a big help, and this job should make things easier. But it's not a decision I took lightly."

Our bodies are inching closer and closer, drawn together by an invisible force. His green eyes are penetrating my hazel ones.

"For what it's worth, I think you made the right decision."

"Yeah? Why?"

"Because… " I trail off, my brain stuttering to a stop simply from being this close to him again.

"Because you're here?"

I can smell the familiar spearmint scent from the mints I remember him being obsessed with. He was always crunching on one. I came to love that flavour, and even now I have a container of the exact same mints in my car. My hand lifts up to lay against his chest, feeling the lines of his uniform and the hard muscle underneath. I let my eyes flutter closed.

"Look at me, Serena."

My body responds willingly, and when I open my eyes, he's right there.

"I need to kiss you." It's barely a whisper, yet I hear — and feel — every word down to my bones. His eyes search mine, and I know he's looking for any hesitation on my part. But he won't find any. Just to make that clear, I lift up onto my toes and press my lips to his.

In so many ways, it's our first kiss. But it's a first kiss laden with history, with familiarity, with old love.

His mouth fits over mine perfectly, and the rhythm we had all those years ago returns instantly. As his tongue slides over the seam of my lips, I part, letting him in. He pulls his hand from mine only to cup my head and tilt slightly, covering even more of me with his lips. It turns greedy and demanding, and I let it happen. Leo can have whatever he wants from me.

But just as I'm about to give in to temptation and attempt to see what's underneath that uniform, I remember reality.

Leo has a daughter, and an ex, and twenty years of life that I know nothing about.

I break away, even though my body aches at the loss of contact. Because no matter how much I want him right now, and he clearly wants me, too, it won't last. It never does.

Chapter Six

Leo

Kissing Serena was not a good idea. It was amazing, but not a good idea. She's still got her walls up high, and I don't know if I can find a way in — or if I even should. After Alexa left, I swore to myself I'd never let anyone else walk out on Violet ever again, and Serena definitely seems like she's got one foot out the door.

When I got off shift this morning, Aunt Claire had already taken my baby girl out for the day so I could sleep.

But rest did not come easy. My head refused to settle, instead flipping between memories of high school with Serena, memories of the first few months with Alexa and Violet, when things seemed like they might actually work out, and then memories of the first few weeks after Alexa left. When I was stuck trying to figure out how to parent a tiny baby by myself.

I don't know if I can trust Serena, even knowing now why she did what she did. I get that her parents' divorce was unexpected, but if that's how she handles big stressors, how would she handle a kid?

When Violet and Aunt Claire return home in the early afternoon, I'm exhausted mentally and physically. But I put on a smile for my girl as she babbles in my ear, stroking my cheek and hugging my arm while we sit on the couch.

"Seems like you had a good day?" I ask Aunt Claire, who's picking up her things.

"We certainly did. We drove over to Westport to check out a playground that has a splash pad for little ones, and Miss Violet had plenty of fun getting Aunt Claire all wet, didn't you?" She leans down to tickle Vi's feet, earning a giggle. "Oh, and while we were there, someone mentioned a farm nearby that has animals, and your little lady was very interested in seeing the P-O-N-Y."

"Got it. Well, maybe that's something we can do this week on my day off. Thanks again for taking her out this morning."

"Of course. Did you get some sleep?"

I wince. "No, but it's fine."

Aunt Claire puts her hands on her hips and arches a brow at me. "Leo Talbot, you're a single father. You need rest."

Tell me something I don't know, I think to myself, but to Aunt Claire, I just smile. "I know. It's fine, I'll go to bed early tonight."

"You're sure you don't want me to come back so you can go out with the boys?"

I stand up with Violet in my arms and guide her to the door. "Yes, I'm sure. It's more than enough that you help when I have to work, you don't need to babysit just so I can go out for a beer."

She lifts her hand to cup my cheek, the gesture mothering in nature. "Your cousins are so happy you're here, and so am I. We *want* to help you find a better balance between being a dad and being yourself."

"Thank you. But I'm good. I'll see you tomorrow?"

Aunt Claire looks at me a moment longer before kissing Violet on the forehead and finally walking out the door.

I love her and she has the best intentions, but Vi is my kid, my responsibility. And that means no nights at the bar for awhile. That's the deal, that's the job. And I take my role of father even more seriously than my role of police officer.

"Alright missy, why don't we grab a snack and then go outside to set up that playhouse for you?"

Later that evening, I get Violet settled for bed surprisingly easily. I guess she was tired out from the day. I'll take it as a win. Just as I'm opening the fridge to see if there's any beer left, a quiet knock sounds at my door.

Opening it reveals three of my five cousins crowded on my front porch. Sawyer's holding a six pack of beer, Max has a bag that looks like chips or something, and Beckett has his hands in his pockets.

"Uh, hey guys, what's going on?"

Sawyer pushes his way past me and heads straight to the kitchen. "Guys night."

Max comes in next and whisper-yells to his brother, "Dude, be quiet, Vi's sleeping." On his way to the kitchen he turns and gives me a nod of his head. "Hey Leo."

Beckett is the only one who stops in the doorway and has the decency to look sheepish. "Sorry to crash in on you like this, but we really wanted to hang out tonight. Hope it's okay?"

I give him a quick smile as we follow his brothers into the kitchen. "So, it's not that I'm *not* happy to see you, but I thought you were going to the pub tonight?"

Sawyer turns to me with a *is this guy stupid* look on his face. "Yeah, we were, if you could come. But since you didn't want Mom to babysit, we figured we'd move guys night here."

"I said we should've warned you," Beckett chimes in. His comment doesn't surprise me. Out of the four guys, he's always been the most responsible and reserved when it comes to social-izing. He's the introvert of the family, an accountant, and often the only voice of reason with his brothers. Especially when it comes to Sawyer. For twins, those two are like night and day with their opposing personalities.

"Yeah, and I said if we did that, old man Leo would find a reason to say no. Better to ask forgiveness than permission and all that shit." Sawyer cracks open a beer and hands it to me before doing the same for his brothers. "Cheers, man." I inwardly roll my eyes. He's the definition of a hotheaded middle child.

"We thought about bringing the poker set but figured we'll save that for another night. It's too nice out to be inside. You got the firepit set up yet?" Max asks, moving to the back door.

"No, but it's quick enough," I reply. We head outside, and Sawyer helps me set up the propane fire pit, insisting he be the one to check the connections. I'm perfectly capable of doing it myself, but I let him do it anyway. Good luck convincing a firefighter not to care about fire safety.

"Did you catch Jude's last game?" Max asks once we're all settled around the fire. The second oldest Donnelly, Jude, is a forward with the Montana Blaze hockey team. He was home briefly around the time I moved here, but now he's on the road playing in the NHL.

"Fuck yeah, he dominated that third period."

The brothers all lift their beers, and we drink to Jude. When he was back, he made a couple of comments about possibly retiring soon. He's in his early thirties, so I would have figured he could keep playing for a while. But Max confided in me that Jude's had a couple of concussions already, and he might need to stop playing before the risk of brain damage gets any higher.

"So. Leo the lion."

Goddamnit, that nickname pisses me off. One Halloween costume as a child and Sawyer never lets me forget it. I suppress my eye roll and give him a questioning glance.

"Rumour around town is that you've been hanging out with Miss Serena, that hottie dance teacher."

Anger flares inside of me at his description of her. "Hey, be a bit more respectful, asshole."

He lifts his hands in apology. "Woah, sorry, sore subject?"

I take a sip of my beer. My cousins all moved away from the town in Ontario we all grew up in before Serena and I got together, so they never met her. Which means they don't know about our history. All of a sudden I realize I could use some perspective. Because they may not know Serena and I have a past, but they might know her now. Which could give me some insight and help me figure out what the fuck to do.

"We dated back in high school." *Now there's an understatement if I ever said one.* "Actually, she was the fucking love of my life until she broke up with me and destroyed me for any other woman," I blurt out.

Silence fills the space after my verbal vomit, and I keep my eyes on the fire as I chug what's left of my beer. "I'm gonna get another. Anyone else?" I stand up, not waiting for their reply, and head into the kitchen. I can't quite believe I just put it all out there like that. Even if these guys are family, that doesn't mean we've ever gotten touchy-feely with our emotions. And I just admitted to having my heart ripped to pieces by a woman they all know. *Fuck.* What if one of them dated her? Sure, they're younger than we are, but age doesn't really matter these days. Grabbing a beer, I march back outside.

"Please tell me none of you jackasses ever made a move on her," I growl and they all immediately shake their heads. "Thank fuck for that." I sink back down into my chair and pop the top off my beer, drinking it down.

"So, you and Serena. That seems like... I dunno, something?" Max asks cautiously.

I nod. "Yeah. It's something."

"And? Come on dude, give us more to go on," Sawyer says impatiently.

"There's not much more to say. We have a past, and for her, that included walking away when shit got tough in her life. Now she's got these walls up, and I don't know if I have the time, the energy, or the desire to try and push through them. Vi's gotta be my priority. Not to mention, I can't take the risk of her deciding to walk away again. Not now, not with Violet. I have to think of more than just myself."

"That's a lot more," Beckett murmurs into the quiet that follows.

"You've been thinking about it, about her."

I don't acknowledge Max's comment. I'd say it's pretty fucking obvious that I've given me and Serena plenty of thought.

"You know Serena's accountant is my partner, Jonas. She's always seemed really grounded and content in Dogwood Cove. Connected to the community and all that. Why are you so worried she'd walk away again?"

I turn to Beckett. "Shit, I don't know. Maybe it has to do with the two women who I figured would have the most invested in staying with me walking out; it kinda jades a guy. And like I said, she's got walls. Strong walls. I don't know if she'd even be interested in trying again."

"Serena is nothing like Alexa."

The mention of Violet's biological mother makes my eye twitch. Any woman that could just up and decide she didn't want to be a mom and walk away from their baby for no better reason than it was cramping their *lifestyle* doesn't deserve a lot of my respect.

"I know she isn't. But I still gotta think of Vi."

"Doesn't Violet deserve a dad who's happy?" Max asks, and damn if his question doesn't hit me square in the heart.

"Of course she does. But my happiness is secondary to hers," I fire back.

"Or maybe your happiness could be found *with* hers."

Lying in bed that night, I flip my phone over and over in my hand, unable to get what Max said out of my head.

Is it even remotely possible that I could make things work with Serena?

More importantly, is it possible that I can live in the same town as her and *not be with her?*

At least I know the answer to the second question.

LEO: Hey, you awake?

SERENA: Yeah

I type without pausing to consider what I'm writing.

LEO: It felt really fucking good kissing you.

LEO: I don't regret it and I sure as shit hope you don't.

I watch those three damn dots travel across the screen for long enough to send my heart rate sky high until finally, I get a response.

SERENA: I don't regret it. I just don't know what to do about it.

LEO: You know what I missed the most about you was your energy. You brought so much life and happiness into my world. It didn't matter how bad my mom's depression was, or how difficult baseball practice was, or what test I failed. Being with you always made me feel better. Feel loved.

SERENA: Leo...

I push the button for a video call and instantly regret it when I see her beautiful face and only the thin straps of a tank top. She's in bed as well, her blonde hair spread over a pillow. Fuck, I wish I was there in person, not doing this over the phone.

"Tippy, I didn't say that to make you feel bad or anything. I just needed to tell you how much you meant to me back then."

A soft, sleepy smile creeps across her face. It feels like I've made a small chink in the defensive wall around her heart. Then she tucks her lower lip between her teeth, and her face fills with uncertainty. I hate seeing that.

"I know that what I did, breaking us up, might make this hard for you to believe, but I felt the same way about you. When I was with you, I was safe, I was loved, I was home. Walking away from that was the hardest thing I ever did, Leo. But at the time," She takes a pause and lets her breath out on a long exhale, laden with emotion. "At the time, I thought it was for the best."

"And what about now," I whisper, my eyes locked on hers through the screen.

"Now I'm not so sure."

Chapter Seven

Serena

Shockingly enough, I fell asleep soon after hanging up with Leo. The comfort I always felt around him when we were younger hasn't changed, and just seeing his face, hearing his voice, was enough to relax my thoughts so I could fall into a deep sleep. Despite the fact that my heart remained tied up in knots.

I want so badly to open up to Leo, to let myself fall and know he'll catch me like he always did. But trusting someone in that way again is terrifying. Especially someone whose heart is already taken by his adorable little girl.

But that's a worry for another time. Today is tiny tot class day, and I keep checking the door to see when Violet comes in. Last class, she shocked me and Claire by running over and giving my legs an adorable hug.

It's almost time for class to begin, and there's no sign of Violet. A part of me is worried she's sick or something's happened, but I don't have time to text Leo to ask. I reluctantly make my way to the front of the studio to get started when the door opens, and Leo himself comes rushing in, Violet in his arms and a harried expression on his face. His eyes fly around the studio full of young mothers and their kids until they land on me.

"Sorry. Aunt Claire isn't feeling well, and none of my cousins are free. I had to duck out of work early and run home to get her."

I make my way to the back of the room where Violet is squirming to be let down and Leo is looking completely lost.

"It's fine," I say. Looking at Violet, I give her a warm smile and she gives a toothy grin right back. "Alright Miss Vi, why don't you go and find a spot in the circle for you and Daddy." As soon as she's out of his arms, I turn my attention to Leo. At least he didn't show up in uniform, although the tight-fitting T-shirt and loose basketball shorts are showing off his athletic body in a different, yet just as sexy, way. I lick my lips and his eyes zero in on the motion. His lips quirk at the corner and I know he can sense my reaction.

Nope. Shut that down. Not while there's a studio full of moms and kids waiting for me.

"You can put your shoes in a cubby and join us when you're ready." I give him a reassuring smile, and he takes a deep breath in and out.

"Thanks. Sorry again that we're late. It's totally my fault."

"Don't worry. Just breathe, and try to have fun."

His lips quirk up slightly. "I don't know if that'll happen. Remember the last time you tried to teach me to dance?"

I bite back my laugh. "This will be different, I promise."

The next forty-five minutes is torture for so many reasons. Leo is adorably awkward but completely focused on Violet, so he doesn't see all the other moms and caregivers eyeing him, but I do. I can't exactly blame them; who wouldn't be attracted to a hunky dad doting on his adorable girl? And when he puts his hands up and goes on his toes to spin in a circle, I swear I hear one of the women swoon. It's a battle to hide my own reactions, especially whenever I get too close to the two of them. It's even more of a battle not to shoot daggers at the ladies going gaga over him.

When the class eventually ends, Leo is swarmed by everyone, all of them gushing over him and how sweet it was for him to bring his daughter. Like it's that big of a deal for a father to do something like this. Sure, it might be more typical for the mom or the nanny to be the one to bring a kid, but he's not the first father to show up to a dance class.

He's just the hottest.

Jealousy burns inside of me at the attention he's getting and giving to them all until a small hand tugs at my skirt.

"Dance wif me?"

I look down to Violet's hopeful face. "Of course, sweet girl. Come with me."

We go over to an open space, and I take her hands as we start to twirl and sway to our own beat. Pretty soon, she's giggling and I'm smiling, and I completely lose track of Leo and the other parents. Until Vi breaks away from me and runs up to him, and he swoops her up into his arms.

"That was beautiful, baby girl."

I realize the studio has emptied, and it's just the three of us.

"Do you want to ask Miss Serena if she'll do a special dance for us?" he asks Violet, his eyes burning into me the entire time.

"Yes!"

"What do you think, Miss Serena, could you show your favourite student a special dance?"

I know what he's asking, but I can't do *that* dance. Not now, not until I've had a chance to prepare myself for the emotions that always bubble up when I dance that piece. The choreography I designed for our song, "I Don't Wanna Miss A Thing" by Aerosmith, is powerful for me. It's the best thing I've ever created, and it comes straight from my heart.

But I can't say no to Violet or her father, it seems. So instead, I line up a different song and take my place at the front of the studio. Leo sits down on the floor near the back and settles Violet in his lap. When the music starts, I close my eyes and let go. I glide across the floor, feeling the power of the music and the movement, and the intense emotional tug of knowing Leo is watching. As my body bends and sways in the motions that are as familiar to me as breathing, I sense the energy in the air changing, building, just like whatever it is between Leo and I. And Violet's an important part of it all. That little girl is changing me, changing us. We can't go back; we can only go forward. The past was then and this is now. And maybe, just maybe, opening up to the possibility of a now with Leo won't be the worst thing in the world.

When the song finishes, I drop into my final pose, and the studio falls quiet for a second before Vi's little voice pops up.

"'Gain? Dance 'gain?"

"No baby, not again. But wasn't Miss Serena amazing?" His voice is hoarse, laden with emotion.

I make my way over to them and sit down cross-legged. I'm breathing heavily, but not so much from exertion, more from the feelings coursing through my body. "I'm glad you liked it, Violet."

She scrambles off her father's lap and to my surprise, launches herself into my lap. Her sweet little arms wrap around my neck. "Fank you."

I squeeze her tightly, relishing the feel of this small child loving and trusting me so deeply. Who knew a simple hug from a three-year-old could be so powerful? "You are so welcome."

Leo clears his throat, and when I look up at him, I'm shocked to see that his eyes almost look watery, like he's about to cry. He stands up and turns away for a second before facing us again.

"Well Violet, we better get going and let Miss Serena get ready for her next class."

"Actually, I have a bit of a break right now."

Violet's arms squeeze me tighter. "Stay."

"Vi, we can't stay, honey."

"Stay!"

Leo looks from his daughter to me, and I can see he's not sure what to do or say right now.

"Why don't we go for a walk outside and see if we can get my friend Mila to give us a treat?"

"Tweat?" Violet's head pops up, and she looks at Leo. "Daddy, tweat?"

"Yes, baby girl, if we go for a walk, we can stop and get a treat at the bakery." He looks at me and mouths "thank you" as he takes Violet's hand, and they head into the outer room where the cubbies are.

I take advantage of the moment alone to take a few deep breaths to clear away the overwhelm that's threatening me. It feels like things are getting serious in a way, with Violet's feelings now clearly entwined with mine and Leo's.

Whatever decisions we make, she's a part of them. If we're together, it's the three of us, not the two of us anymore. That's a really big freaking deal.

When I've changed my shoes and swapped my dance skirt for something a bit more appropriate to walk around town, I meet Leo and Violet outside the studio. Vi reaches for my hand and we head down the sidewalk. Leo looks at me over her head and the look of yearning on his face is matched by my own, I'm sure. Something about this simple action of walking hand in hand with him and his daughter is stirring up desires in my heart that I'd long since put aside.

"How's your mom?"

Leo flashes me a quick smile. "She's good. She'll be thrilled to hear you live in Dogwood Cove. You know, she was so mad at me when we broke up."

I stumble over nothing, my eyes finding his. "What?"

He just laughs. "Yeah, she figured it was all my fault and told me I was a moron for letting the best girl around get away."

My mouth is flapping open like a freaking guppy fish.

"Tippy, chill. She loves you, that's all."

"But I feel bad," I say lamely. "It wasn't your fault at all, Leo."

Leo pulls us to a stop and fixes me with a stern look. "It doesn't matter now and it didn't matter then. Mom was right, you are the best girl around. And she's gonna be so happy to know I found you again."

He starts walking again, Violet skipping along between us, oblivious to the fact that I am so freaking mixed up inside. I miss Leo's mom. She was such an amazing woman when she wasn't in the trenches of her grief. Hearing that she had no idea what went on in my family is confusing, but then again, my parents kept things pretty quiet. And after I left for school, Mom moved away, too. So maybe news just never made it back to the Talbot house.

We reach the green space in the center of Dogwood Cove and Violet breaks free, running ahead on her little legs to the gazebo. She climbs the steps and starts to spin around.

"Seeing you with her," Leo says, then stops, shoving his hands in the pockets of his shorts. "Fuck. I don't know how to say it."

"Just say it," I whisper.

"It's like a dream come true, but a dream I never knew I wanted. And then I feel so much regret that we missed out on this. Add in my anger at Alexa for walking away from her daughter, and then gratitude that she *did* walk away because it led me — led us — to you." He lets out a low laugh. "It's messed up. I know."

"It's not messed up. It sounds super familiar, honestly."

He glances over at me, his mouth open in surprise. "Really?"

I nod and take one of his hands out of his pocket so I can weave our fingers together. "Yeah, really. I wanted this with you. A life, a family with you. I know you had your reasons for not wanting that, and I truly believed I could have given up my dream of being a mother. Which is why seeing that you found it with someone else hurts, even though she isn't around. It hurts because I did this to us. I broke us. I'm the reason you had a child with someone who wasn't me." I pause, thinking through what I need to say next. "But then at the same time, that gratitude you feel? I feel it in a way, as well. Because Violet is amazing. And I can't begrudge you for being with her mom at all, because Vi was the end result."

His mouth is on mine before I can take a breath, and even though it's a short kiss, it's no less powerful.

"Thank you," he breathes, his forehead on mine.

I want to ask why he's thanking me, but our moment is interrupted by Violet running up to us, a fistful of dandelions in her hand.

"Fowlers!"

"Wow, look at those flowers, Vi, they're so pretty." Leo bends down and picks up his daughter, kissing her cheek. "But not as pretty as you are."

Violet twists in his arms to face me, and holds out her hand with the flowers in it. "Pwetty fowlers, Rena."

The way she says my name and the fact that it's the first time she said it makes my heart melt into a puddle of goo. "Thank you so much, Violet. They're lovely." I take the flowers and try not to let the tears that are threatening to spill over.

"Tweat now?"

"Yeah, baby. Let's go get a treat." Leo shifts her onto one side and reaches out with his hand to me. Taking it feels momentous, somehow. And walking across the grass to The Nutty Muffin, something's changed inside of me.

Some invisible force has decided for me that I can't walk away from this man and his daughter.

CHAPTER EIGHT

Leo

The day after taking Violet to dance class, I put my plan into action.

Operation Convince Serena to Give Me Another Chance.

It's a long name, but it's the best I can do.

"I don't suppose you know what's Serena's favourite thing to eat?" I ask my cousin Kat while picking up my lunch from Camille's café.

"Ooh, the pretty dance teacher? She either gets a chef's salad or the prosciutto panini." Kat grins at me widely, making me slightly regret involving her. "Why you asking, cuz? Trying to win her over?"

"More like trying to win her back," I mutter, glancing around to see who might overhear. "Keep it between us though, okay?"

Kat mimes zipping her lips. "You got it. Secret is safe. But if you really want to woo her, you should go next door and get her a macaroon bar. Mila just created them last week and I heard Serena moaning about how good they were."

An image of Serena moaning underneath me pops into my head, and I have to stifle my reaction to that.

"Thanks, Kat. Can you get the sandwich ready while I go and get one?"

Ten minutes later, I push the door open to the studio. A check of the schedule that Aunt Claire has oh so helpfully put on my fridge at home revealed she's got a break in classes right now, and as luck would have it, I was able to time my lunch break for the same hour she has off.

"Tippy? You in here?"

"Leo?" She comes around the corner and my greedy eyes drink in the sight of her in her dance clothes. A filmy short skirt covers a deep purple leotard, but her legs are bare except for ballet slippers on her feet. Her beauty is breathtaking, and it hits me like a punch to the gut, the warmth spreading throughout my body.

"I was hoping to join you for lunch," I say, holding up the bag. When her face melts into a smile, I feel light inside. I forgot how good it feels to make this woman smile.

"That would be amazing. Do you want to come upstairs?" She gestures to a door off to the side. "I actually live up there."

"Nice commute," I tease, earning a soft giggle. Serena locks the door to the studio and flips over a sign that reads *Be Back Soon*, then I follow her up the staircase, trying not to stare too hard at her perfectly round ass. Then again, who could blame me when it's right in front of me and covered in just two thin layers of fabric. While she's focused on the space in front of her,

I subtly adjust myself, for once grateful for the stiff material of my uniform.

She opens a door at the top of the stairs and I step in after her, taking a look around. The entire space is so quintessential Serena. Soft fabric drapes over the window, the small couch is covered in colourful pillows and blankets, and there's a random mix of eclectic furniture and lamps. It's like a chaotic explosion of happy energy.

Serena goes into the kitchen and comes back with two plates. "Do you want something to drink?"

"Water's fine. I'm still on shift."

When she's back with two glasses, she sits down on the couch, folding her legs underneath her. I sit close, but not touching, and take the food out of the bag.

"How did you know that's my favourite sandwich?" she says when I hand her the panini.

"My cousin helped," I admit with a shrug.

"Oh yeah. I can't believe your cousins have been here in town this whole time and I had no idea." Her words hold the slightest tinge of remorse, and I'm weirdly happy she's disappointed about missing how closely we were connected for at least some of our time apart.

"Apparently, her older brother works at the accounting firm you use, as well."

"Yeah, he does. I'm surprised I never noticed the family re-semblance, although it's not that obvious." Serena shakes her head, then takes a bite of her sandwich, letting out a hum of satisfaction. "Mmm, this is so good."

Her finger comes up to wipe at a bit of sauce on the corner of her mouth. Fuck, do I ever want to lean over and lick it off.

"Glad you're enjoying it." Christ, my voice is hoarse, my dick is hard, and all she did was take a bite of a sandwich. I know it's been a ridiculously long time since I had sex, but this is nuts.

No, this is how I've always reacted to Serena. She has a direct line to my sex drive. I'm completely helpless against my physical reaction to her. We were insatiable as teenagers, always wanting more from each other, and it only got worse after we finally had sex for the first time, our final year of high school. We'd been dating for over a year, messing around constantly. But once that line was crossed, we couldn't keep our hands off each other or our clothes on.

"Do you remember that one school dance we went to when Jay Potter spiked the punch?" she asks, smirking at me.

I groan. Because yes, I do remember. "You mean the one when I was dared to race him in how many cups we could drink in a minute, and I ended up puking in the garbage can because I didn't *know* the punch was spiked? Yeah. I remember. Why?"

She lifts one shoulder delicately. "I don't know. That night is just one I remember."

"I remember it for another reason," I say quietly. Her eyes meet mine, and I'm transported back to that night where we danced under the cheesy strobe lights of a high school dance, and I told Serena I loved her for the first time.

"Yeah. I remember that, too." She looks down at the sandwich in her hand, then back up to me. "I was so desperate for you to say it first, but I'd been waiting what felt like forever for you to do it. I wanted to tell you so badly that I loved you, but all my friends said I had to wait."

Her confession makes me chuckle. "Seriously? And there I was panicking that it was too soon, that I'd scare you away. I almost didn't say it that night."

Her hand rests on my leg, and the heat emanating from her is matched by the one burning inside of me. When she takes her hand away, I feel the loss of her touch as an ache inside. I've missed her so fucking much.

We finish lunch, reminiscing about high school, keeping the memories light and away from anything emotional. When she takes the last bite of her sandwich, I reach into the bag and pull out a small box with The Nutty Muffin logo on it.

"Ooh, dessert?" Serena licks her lips.

I open the box, revealing the bar that Kat said Serena loves. "Word on the street is that these make you moan."

Her eyes widen at the not-so-subtle innuendo in my words, and she nods slowly. "One of the few pleasures I have in life right now is Mila's baking."

"If baked goods are the source of your pleasure, you need to expand your horizons."

"Well, they're not the *only* source. A girl's gotta do what a girl's gotta do."

"True."

"That's why vibrators were invented, after all. To make up for the shortcomings of men."

I choke on my sip of water. Holy fuck.

"Shortcomings? That tells me you haven't been with a talented enough guy in a while."

"Nope. Not for about twenty years, give or take."

We're staring at each other, both of us breathing heavily. The door is open for me to make a move, but she's not ready. Not the way I want her to be — emotionally, not just physically. When I get her back in bed, I want all of her. Heart, soul, body.

And I know I've made the right call when she turns to face the table and picks up her own water, drinking it all until the glass is empty.

"Can I have a taste?" I ask in a low, gravelly voice.

Serena lifts the bar out of the bakery box and holds it up to my mouth. I lean in, keeping my eyes trained on her and take a bite.

It's delicious.

But I bet she would taste even better. Serena takes a bite, and sure enough, her eyes close and a soft moan escapes her.

The situation in my pants gets even harder. God, that sound. I missed that sound. I can feel my self-control slipping, but I'm saved by the squawk of the radio on my shoulder. It's nothing important, just a check-in from an officer on patrol, but the heated moment between Serena and me is broken, nonetheless.

"I should probably head back to the station. I've got some calls to make and then a staff meeting in an hour," I say, standing up and collecting our dishes before carrying them over to the kitchen.

Serena follows, and my body takes notice of how close she stands next to me. "Thank you for lunch."

I shift slightly so that I can lean against the counter next to her, and gauging her reaction, slowly lift my hand up to tuck a few strands of hair behind her ear. "You're welcome."

I can see the desire brimming in her eyes, but it's still laced with hesitation. Our flirting helped lower some of her walls, but she's not there yet. I settle for moving my hand to the back of her neck and gently tugging her in close enough to lightly kiss her cheek.

"Have a good afternoon, Tippy."

My restraint is rewarded by a quiet, feminine growl, and then Serena grabs my face and pulls my mouth down to meet hers. Our tongues tangle together instantly as she opens to me, meeting stroke for stroke. I wrap my hands around her waist and lift her up, her legs moving to wrap around my waist.

"Ouch." She pulls back and we both look down. "It's your, uh... "

"My gun. Shit. Sorry." Our foreheads drop together as we both laugh at the insanity of the moment. I turn us so that I can set her down on the counter. Careful of where my duty belt might hit her, I lean in and kiss her again, lingering over her lips. Her hands come up to play in my hair, but the beeping of the calendar alert on my phone interrupts us.

"That's my cue. I really need to go," I murmur. We separate and I lift my thumb to swipe across Serena's swollen lips. "Fuck, you're beautiful." Her hands come to my chest and she pushes me back a step.

"You're just saying that because I let you kiss me," she teases, her hazel eyes dancing. "But I only kissed you to thank you for lunch."

"Uh huh." I smirk. "If that's how you thank me for lunch, what do I get if I take you to dinner sometime?"

"Guess you'll have to wait and see."

I let out a fake groan as we make our way downstairs. "You're torturing me." At the door to the studio, I pause. "But does that mean you'll let me take you out on a real date?"

She tilts her head to the side and the corners of her mouth lift slightly. "I'd like that."

Leaning in, I kiss her briefly one more time. "Good. I'll call you later."

For the next few days, I try to make a point of doing small things to show Serena I'm thinking of her. I fill the tires on her car with air when I notice one looking a little low, and I drop off peppermint tea the night she has an evening class. When I see a package of licorice at the store, I remember that she used to buy them every time we'd go to the movies, so I leave a package on the desk at the front of the studio one afternoon while she's teaching.

We haven't been able to spend any real time together since our lunch date. But tonight I'm pulling another night patrol shift to help out and it's quiet. When a familiar song comes on the radio, it inspires me, and half an hour later I drive past the studio. The lights are off, but they're on upstairs in her apartment. Opening my phone, I send an email attachment, then type out a quick text.

LEO: check your email...

SERENA: Why, did you send me nudey booty photos?

"What the fuck?" I laugh, but then the thought of Serena sending nude photos or even worse *receiving* nude photos from someone hits me.

LEO: No. Why. Is that something that happens often?

Damn it, Leo, way to sound like a possessive caveman.

LEO: Forget I said that. Sorry.

LEO: No I didn't send you... whatever you called them.

SERENA: LOL. Boooo.

SERENA: For the record, no. Never sent 'em, never received 'em.

A surge of relief fills me, followed closely by a carnal curiosity.

LEO: Would you ever? Send them that is?

SERENA: Guess it depends on who's receiving...

LEO: Good point.

I watch the "..." appear and disappear a couple of times, and I can't deny the anticipation that builds in me. When her message finally pops up, it's sort of a let down, even though it shouldn't be.

SERENA: So, my email. Give me a sec

It's so hard to figure out how hard I can push the flirtation with her right now. So instead, I wait for her to open my email, hoping she likes it. And also, hoping it doesn't look too conspicuous having a cop car parked out front of her studio for so long. All the other times I've stopped by for any length of time, it's been daytime and I've just walked over. But tonight I need to be patrolling, which means the very obvious cop car.

SERENA: Leo...

SERENA: Omg. It's all of our songs. I love it. Thank you.

LEO: You're welcome. Maybe someday you'll dance to Aerosmith for me again.

SERENA: Maybe someday.

LEO: Good night Tippy.

SERENA: Good night Leo.

As I pull away, I press play on the very playlist I sent to her, filled with the soundtrack to our teenage love. I skip ahead to the song we used to slow dance to in my mom's basement, the song Serena choreographed a dance to for a solo competition she won.

And as Steven Tyler starts singing about how he *don't wanna miss a thing*, I realize I don't, either. Not anymore.

Chapter Nine

Serena

"Amals!" Violet screeches from the backseat for the tenth time this morning. The drive to the farm that Abby and her uncle own isn't long, but apparently even a short drive can feel infinitely longer when you've got an impatient toddler in the vehicle. That alone was eye-opening for me about what life with kids is truly like. Strangely enough, I kind of love it. Her energy is infectious and reminds me of myself sometimes.

"Yes, baby girl, animals. We're going to see the animals," Leo says calmly, just as he has every time she's gotten a little too loud and excited. He turns to me with an apologetic glance. "Sorry, I know she's a lot right now, but anything to do with animals and you'd never know she's normally so shy."

I simply smile back at Violet who's babbling to herself in her car seat. "It's fine, Leo. I love how excited she is."

When Leo texted me the other day to ask if I knew anything about the Martin family farm and how he wanted to take Violet to see the animals on his upcoming day off, I saw a way to spend time with him, but with a buffer. A quick phone call to Abby and I had a special surprise lined up for Violet today.

It seemed like the least I could do after everything he's been doing for me. The truth is, I forgot how sweet and considerate Leo can be. But this past week, with all the little things he's done for me, it's obvious he's trying to woo me. And he's wooing hard.

He's slowly chipping away at the defenses around my heart, which I know is exactly his intention. He's making his feelings about me — about us — clear, and I'm finding it harder and harder to deny my own. I want him and more importantly, I want to let myself love him.

I'm normally loud and proud about my independence and how I don't need a partner in life because I can take care of myself better anyway. But this week, Leo's pointing out the little ways that having someone who cares for you in a romantic way can just make life better.

Which leads to now. The proximity to him in this small, confined space has been an exquisite form of torture. The air is a mix of spearmint and a fresh, woodsy smell that is undeniably Leo. The sun coming in through the window catches the blonde hairs on his muscular forearms as he grips the steering wheel, and it is physically painful not to reach out and touch him when he's this close. A couple of times his hand flexed and I thought he was going to reach for me, but we're both resisting contact. It helps, somehow, to know he's as conflicted as I am about what to do.

"So, remind me again how you know the people that own the farm? I need to start memorizing who's who around here."

I shift back into my seat with a small smile. Something about hearing Leo talk about settling down in Dogwood Cove warms me inside.

"Reid Corser is the elementary school principal and one of Ethan's best friends. He grew up here, just like Ethan and Mila. Abby's uncle, Steve, owns the farm. When he broke his leg last winter, she came to town to help out, fell in love with Reid, and never left. So now she lives here on the farm with Reid, her uncle, and her daughter Layla."

"Got it."

A few minutes later, we pull up in front of the large farmhouse on the Martin family farm property. Violet starts bouncing up and down in her seat, shrieking random noises, and I can see why. Abby's prepared for us and has the goats and chickens roaming free in the space in front of the house and a miniature pony already saddled up. Leo turns to me, an indiscernible look on his face.

"Did you set all of this up for Vi?"

I nod, suddenly unsure if I overstepped.

"Serena," he starts, then stops, and I watch his throat move as he swallows. "Thank you." Our eyes are like opposing magnets, pulled together by an invisible force.

Abby's moved closer to the truck now and I see her out of the corner of my eye. "We should get Violet out of her seat."

Leo shifts as if coming out of a trance and I know the feeling. "Yeah. Right."

We get out, Abby staring at me questioningly, but I avoid her gaze. "Okay, do we want to ride the pony first, or see the animals?"

"Amals!" Vi screeches, beelining for one of the goats placidly munching on grass by the side of the house.

"Goats it is," I say, following after her. Leo and Abby hold back, I'm guessing to discuss the pony ride, as I meander after the toddler who's babbling at the goats. They're being remarkably patient with her grabby hands, but I guess they're used to kids.

"Hey Violet, want to feed one?"

The little girl turns to me, nodding wildly, and I pull out the bag of pellet food Abby gave me when we arrived. Sprinkling some in my hand, I crouch down and show her how the goat nibbles it out of my palm.

"Me do."

"Yup, you do it this time." I pour a little food onto her palm and carefully help hold her hand out flat. Her shriek of laughter when the goat starts eating makes me smile.

"'Gain, 'gain!"

"Okay, sweetie. Here we go."

Violet and I spend several minutes feeding the goats until I feel a hand stroke across my shoulders.

"Hey, beautiful girls, what are you two up to?"

"Feed amals," Violet announces to her dad. "Daddy feed amals."

Leo chuckles and holds out his hand for some feed. His eyes meet mine over the top of Violet's head and something passes between us.

It would be so easy to start picturing this as my life. Weekend adventures with Leo and Violet, her little hand in mine and her adorable babble filling my ear. It's tempting. It's everything I haven't let myself admit I wanted for the last twenty years. Leo and I talked about kids, in as much as he was adamant he didn't want them, and I thought maybe I did. I always figured there was ample time to make that decision. Children wouldn't be a possibility while I had my dance career, so it wasn't a big deal to back away from our disagreement. But I always wanted to be a mom. With Leo.

But that's a dangerous path. If life has taught me anything, it's that things are often too good to be true. Leo with an adorable little girl, living in Dogwood Cove? I just don't know how to trust that this, too, isn't going to disappear on me eventually.

I stand up and hand the bag of feed to Leo. "I'm just going to talk to Abby for a bit." Hurrying away before he can respond, I find Abby over by the barn tying the pony up to a fence post.

"Hey girl, I see why everyone was excited about your man, he is handsome!"

I wince, and Abby, of course, notices.

"Uh oh. What did I say wrong?" She comes around the pony to the side where I'm standing, slowly stroking the docile creature's soft nose.

"He's not my man. Not anymore."

"Okaaay," Abby says, stretching the word out. "Do you want him to be? Because from what I could see, that guy is definitely interested in picking up wherever you left off."

Hope flares to life inside of me. "Really?"

Abby nods. "Oh heck, yes. He watched you walk after his little girl, and I swear hearts were circling his head. He still has it bad for you."

"I broke his heart, Abby. I don't know if he'll trust me again. Heck, I don't know if I trust me again, or him, or this, or anything!"

"Woah, slow down, Serena." Abby lifts her hands to my shoulders, forcing me to face her. "You're overthinking this. Whatever happened in the past is in the past. Right?"

I nod.

"Okay, then. He trusts you with his daughter, right?"

I nod again.

"Alright, so all that's left is you trusting yourself. What's that all about? This isn't the Serena who takes life by the balls and runs the world," she asks gently. But my walls are rigidly in place.

"It's nothing," I say stiffly. "You're right. I'm overthinking things. Sorry to freak out on you like that."

Abby holds me in place for another second, and I think she's going to question me on my obvious lies, but thank God, she doesn't. Her hands drop away and she takes a step back. "Okay, it's fine. Why don't we show Violet the piglets."

We make our way back over to Leo and Violet, who is surrounded by goats clamouring for affection and treats. She's giggling up a storm, and Leo is the happiest and most relaxed I've seen him since first running into him in town. It's obvious that his little girl is his entire world.

I'm not wrong to wonder if I could actually fit in there somehow or if I'd always be on the outside looking in. And even if it did work out, Violet would always come first. As she should; as is right. But if my own father could abandon me, if my parents' seemingly perfect relationship could fail, if my dream, my passion of dancing could be taken away from me, then why would letting myself fall in love with Leo — for a second time — be any different?

What proof do I have that love could ever work out?

The rest of the morning is a blur for me. I wish I could say that I enjoy every second of witnessing Violet's joy around the animals, but the truth is, I'm stuck in my own head. I know Abby notices, and so does Leo. At least he's too busy with his daughter to ask me about it.

Yet even my withdrawn mood can't stand up to Violet's exuberance when she finally got to ride Archie the pony. Especially when she refuses to have Abby lead the horse and insisted I do it instead. Her excitement is palpable, and the way she reaches over from Leo's arms to hug Archie around the neck after her ride is absolutely precious. My face hurts from smiling so much by the time we're done.

When we're finally in the truck driving back to town, Violet's babble erases any potentially awkward conversations at first. Until, that is, she falls fast asleep five minutes into the drive.

"Thank you again for organizing this, Tippy. I haven't seen her that happy in a long time," Leo says quietly. "And I haven't seen her so connected with someone else, someone who isn't family, I mean, ever."

I bite my lip, torn over how to respond. But Leo beats me to it.

"But don't think I didn't notice you pull away. I know you, Serena. And I know when you disconnect and get stuck in that beautiful head of yours." He pauses and I hold my breath, waiting to see what he'll say next. "I know I don't have any right to ask this... I mean, we're not together. But we are, I think, friends. And as friends, I'm really hoping you'll let me in and tell me what freaked you out all of a sudden."

I wished Violet was my baby girl, that we were together. A family.

And that terrified me.

"Oh, it's nothing. Sorry if I worried you. I just suddenly remembered an issue I'm having with one of my dance classes." The lie rolls off my tongue easily but sounds as hollow as it is. Out of the corner of my eye, I see Leo's hands tighten on the steering wheel. I can't escape the guilt I feel over lying to him, but I also can't see any way to ever tell him the truth.

I miss him, I want him, I want us again. But it'll never be the same — not only because of Violet, but because of us. We're not the starry-eyed teenagers we once were. We've lived our lives, experienced heartache, pain, grief, and it's changed us both.

"Right. Dance."

It doesn't take a genius to read between the lines of those two words. His tone, his body language, everything screams at me that he knows I'm full of shit.

"What happened to Violet's mom?" I ask. Based on Leo's forced exhale, he wasn't expecting me to shift the conversation that way, and for a second I think he's going to push back and try to force the truth from me.

"She decided she didn't want to be a mom anymore somewhere around Vi's three month birthday. I guess no sleep and a colicky baby didn't fit in with her lifestyle."

"Seriously?" I almost shout but remember the sleeping angel in the back seat. "She just walked away from her own daughter?"

Leo nods, his lips a thin line. "Yeah, she handed me paperwork that signed full custody over to me, then packed up and left. We haven't heard from her since."

"Leo, I'm so sorry. You must have been devastated."

He snorts and my eyes widen in surprise at his disdainful reaction.

"Not really. Alexa wasn't the person I wanted to be with, or some great love or anything. She was a one-night stand with a condom that failed. I convinced her we should try and make it work for the baby, but the truth is, her leaving was a relief. She was miserable to be around throughout her pregnancy. It was clear she didn't want Violet, and hell, at first, I wasn't sure I did. That all changed, though, as I realized the baby growing inside of her was mine. A part of me that no one else would ever be. I guess I foolishly thought she'd change her mind when the baby was born. You know, fall in love with her kid or something. But no, she walked away and didn't look back."

A heavy silence fills the car when he finishes.

"Wow. I...I don't know what to say."

He darts a quick look at me, then reaches a hand over and places it on my leg.

"You don't need to say anything. Like I said, I'm hoping we can at least be friends. And friends should know the shit each other has been through. That's how we can try to trust again, to let people in again."

The accuracy of his statement hits me deeply, and the subtext is not lost. He's calling me out on my own lies *and* saying he wants to try again. Try what? I don't know and I don't think he does. But something. His openness makes me want to be truthful.

"Thank you for telling me. I...wasn't exactly honest earlier. About what freaked me out at the farm."

Leo's hand finds mine, and he threads our fingers together. I stare down at our hands, the sight both familiar and new at the same time.

"I know you weren't, Tippy. It's okay. When you're ready, I'm here."

"I'm scared, Leo."

His hand squeezes mine. "Me too. But the fact that you live in the same town as my family, the same town I decide to move to raise my daughter; I can't ignore that. It feels like fate is handing us another chance to get it right."

"But what if we don't get it right," I whisper, unable to hold back from voicing my fear.

All of a sudden, Leo pulls the truck over to the side of the road. My eyes look back, but Violet is fast asleep.

He turns the engine off and opens his door, climbing out. I'm frozen, confused, until he opens my door.

"Get out."

I do so, only because there's no anger or malice in his words, nothing but my gentle Leo in front of me, holding out his hands. I take them and he pulls me into his chest, resting his chin on the top of my head like he used to.

"Serena Matheson. You were — damn it, you still *are* — the love of my life. And I'm fucking terrified to admit that to you, so you're not the only one who's scared." He pulls back slightly and cups my chin. "But aren't you at least a tiny bit curious to see where this could go? We've been given a second chance, Tippy. Take as much time as you need to think about it and figure out if you want to, but you need to know — I do want to. I want everything with you."

His lips meet mine in the briefest whisper of a kiss before pressing more firmly into my forehead.

"You don't have to say anything right away. I just needed to hold you when I told you that."

He releases me and walks back to the truck, leaving me frozen in place, overwhelmed, and just a tiny bit turned on by his swoon-worthy confession.

I seriously need to get my head on straight. And fast. Because while Leo seems all in on this second chance at what might have been, I'm more mixed up and scared than ever.

Chapter Ten

Leo

"Leo, great to see you again. Thanks for taking this meeting."

Ethan and I shake hands, and I take a seat in a chair across from him. We're meeting to discuss the fall festival that's coming up, more specifically, the role for the police. Apparently, managing the security for one of the town's festivals is part of my job description now. Gotta love small towns.

"No problem. I'll be frank, Ethan, I've never coordinated something like this. It's not exactly common for the city police to be so heavily involved; normally, the event organizers would hire private security and we would just patrol."

Ethan laughs. I like the guy, he's my age, and very down-to-earth for a town mayor.

"Around here, everyone wears a lot of hats, and security seemed a natural fit for the police force."

"Oh, agreed, it makes total sense. I just hope you can fill me in a bit more on what to expect." I pull out a notepad and pen. "How many people normally attend, what hours are we looking at, do we need to secure the site before and after or just during, those kinds of things."

He nods and sits up straighter, leaning forward to place his arms on the desk. "You've already given it some thought. I like that. Tell me, how are you and your daughter settling in?"

The shift in conversation takes me by surprise. I came here for work, not personal matters. But if I've learned anything these last few weeks, it's that people around here genuinely care about each other, and that means, no matter what, they take the time to make conversation. It's been an adjustment slowing down like that, but I enjoy it.

"So far, so good. Violet and my aunt have been exploring the area; she loved the Martin farm. It's nice having my family around."

"And she's taking dance classes with my friend Serena. Is it true you guys know each other?"

Ah. I get it. This isn't just a personal chat, this is a *check up on the new guy* chat.

"Yeah, we have a history."

"She's an amazing woman."

"She is."

"Look dude, I don't want to sound like some ridiculous overbearing ass. I made that mistake with Paige when she and Wyatt first hooked up and got shit for it from my sister and my fiancée. So I'll cut the crap. Treat her well, okay? Everyone's really happy to have you in town, and if you and Serena work something out, great. But if you hurt her, it's going to make it awkward and bad for everyone. So just don't."

I stare at him, unblinking for a moment. It's my cop stare, perfected to the point of making most people crack. Sure enough, he starts shifting in his seat, so I break eye contact with an easy grin. "Ethan, I have no idea who Paige and Wyatt are, but believe me on this. I have no intention at all of doing anything but treating Serena the very best I can. Our history is not mine alone to share, but let's just say I'm hoping to have more than just *history* with her."

Ethan lets out a chuckle. "Shit, I can see why you're a good cop. And sorry. I forgot you might not know everyone yet. Hey, why don't you come out to Hastings for a drink tonight after your shift? Everyone's meeting up; we try to get together at least once or twice a month."

"Thanks for the invite, but I need to go and relieve my aunt who's babysitting."

"No worries. The invitation is always open. I'm sure Serena can let you know when we're heading to Hastings. If it works better with your schedule, some friends and I go trail running every Monday afternoon. You're also welcome to join us if that's your kind of thing."

"That could actually work sometime, yeah."

"Cool. Okay, let's get this festival stuff out of the way."

When I get home from work, Aunt Claire informs me that I'm to get changed and head over to her house for a family dinner. Given how tired I am, the idea of not having to cook sounds pretty damn good, and there's a space at my aunt's house where Violet can go to sleep if it gets late, so it's an easy decision to say *yes, please*.

When we get to my aunt and uncle's house, three of my five cousins are there already. Kat is in the kitchen mixing up some sort of potato salad that smells amazing, and Max and Beckett are outside with my Uncle Dennis.

"Is Sawyer on shift?" I ask Kat as I set down Violet and watch her toddle over to the basket of toys Aunt Claire keeps in the corner for when we visit.

"Yeah, he's on nights tonight and tomorrow. He's pissed to be missing dinner tonight," she replies as she pivots to the fridge and pulls out a tray. "We made ribs."

"Oh, hell yeah." My mouth instantly starts to water. Aunt Claire's ribs were famous when we were younger, and I haven't had them in years. "Okay, what can I do to help?"

"Nothing. These go on the grill to caramelize the sauce and then we eat."

"Hey, Leo! Grab a couple beers and come on outside." Max sticks his head through the door. "Hey, baby Vi, how's it going, little peanut?"

Violet looks at him but says nothing, then goes back to her toys.

"Well, she looked at me. I count that as progress. We'll be best friends in no time." Max grins.

"Yeah, until I take her to you for her immunizations and she realizes Uncle Max gives her owies."

"Hey man, don't ruin my progress. We've got time before I have to poke her. Anyway. Beers, outside, now. Let's go. You need to help me convince Beckett to join our rec soccer team. I'd ask you, but the practices are all at night which doesn't work with the peanut."

I grab four beers from the fridge and follow him outside, handing one to him as I go. "Soccer was never my sport anyway. Wrong kind of ball."

"That's right, you were all about baseball, weren't you?"

"You know it." Max clinks his bottle with mine and we take a drink as Uncle Dennis and Beckett wander over.

"Hey Leo, how was work today?

I hand Uncle Dennis a beer before I answer. "Well, it's no hotbed of crime, but Dogwood Cove is an interesting place to work, that's for certain."

"Oh yeah? Did you help some old ladies cross the street?" Beckett teases.

"No," I chuckle. "But I did have a riveting meeting with the mayor about security for the fall fair." I consciously avoid sharing the part where Ethan basically asked me for my intentions with Serena. No need to involve my nosy family in *that* just yet.

"Ethan's a cool guy," Max comments. "I've joined him and his friends for their weekly trail run a time or two."

"He mentioned that. I might try to go if I can squeeze an extra hour or two out of Aunt Claire for babysitting."

"What are you trying to get out of Aunt Claire?" The woman in question comes outside with Violet on her hip and Kat following behind.

"Daddy. Fowler, Rena?" Violet squirms in my aunt's arms, and as soon as she sets her down, Violet beelines for a dandelion growing in the grass and plucks it.

"You want to give that one to Serena, too? I don't know if we'll see her tonight, baby girl."

"Fowler, Rena." Vi's lower lip starts to jut out.

"Here honey, why don't we put your beautiful flower in some water, and you and I can take it to Miss Serena tomorrow," Aunt Claire swiftly interjects, taking Violet by the hand and leading her inside, looking over her shoulder to wink at me as she goes. Something tells me my amazing aunt will be picking a fresh dandelion tomorrow.

Aunt Claire and Violet come back outside, and Vi makes a beeline for me. "Up, Daddy. Pwease."

I lift her up and her arms wrap around my neck as she snuggles in. This right here makes all the stress, all the sleepless nights, all the constant worry worth it. The love I get from my daughter is the purest, most amazing feeling in the world.

If I had someone to share that love with me? That would be... I don't even know how to describe it.

Over dinner, conversation flows amongst us easily. I missed this all these years. The ease of family, the conversation, teasing at times, heartfelt at others. It makes me wonder why I never bothered to come and visit them before now.

If I had, maybe I would have discovered Serena living here, on the same side of the country, a short ferry ride away from me all along.

But then, as Serena said, if we'd found each other before now, there's a chance Violet wouldn't have been created. And that's something I don't want to think about. I may not often feel like I'm doing everything right or being the parent that she needs, but I'm the only one she's got.

I'm in the middle of wiping ice cream off Violet's face when Kat says something that makes me shoot daggers at her.

"So, how did lunch go with Serena?"

"Lunch? When did this happen?" Aunt Claire perks up. Great. And here I figured I had some more time before her matchmaking kicked in.

Beckett's laughing under his breath at me, so I turn my glare on him. Bastard, he should be grateful I'm taking the heat off him and his brothers.

"It's not a big deal. I took her a sandwich from Camille's and we ate together. That's all."

"Did you reminisce about the good ole days?"

That's it. Kat is officially dead to me.

"Good ole days? What is she talking about, Leo. Do you know Serena?"

Taking a deep breath to steel myself against the inevitable, I face my aunt. "We dated in high school."

"Oh, that's so sweet," Aunt Claire swoons, clutching her hands to her chest. It's all I can do not to roll my eyes. But then again, she's not wrong. It is kind of sweet that I just happened to move to the same town as her. "When are you going to take her out on a proper date?"

"I don't know."

"Well, you had better figure it out. And when you do, let me know so I can stay with the little miss. Maybe she can even come here for a sleepover." Aunt Claire raises her eyebrows at me, but I avoid her gaze.

"I wasn't going to ask you to do more, you already spend so much time with her."

"Leo, I adore that little girl. And you need time to be a man, not just a dad. Whether it's drinks with your cousins or a night out with a beautiful woman, you deserve to live your life."

"Here, here." Beckett raises his glass. "Next guys night, no excuses."

"Fine, fine," I grumble before giving my aunt a small smile. "Thanks, Aunt Claire. I do appreciate everything you're doing for us."

Her nod of satisfaction makes it abundantly clear to me that not only is she expecting me to take her up on the offer soon, if I don't, she's gonna give me hell for it.

Later that night, after I get a very sleepy Violet tucked into bed with promises that she and Aunt Claire can take the dandelion to Miss Serena tomorrow, I sink down into one of the

Adirondack chairs I bought for the back deck and pull out my phone.

Despite the fact that I've already essentially professed my love to Serena, I'm nervous about taking the next step.

She could say no to me, to us. She could decide to let her fears overrule what I know she really wants. She could walk away from me again. Only this time, she'd also be walking away from Violet.

I drop my phone on the table in front of me and let my head hang down. Because that right there is the problem. How do I do what's right for my daughter when I have no way of knowing what that actually is? Not for the first time since Vi was born, I think of my dad. What I wouldn't give for him to be here, giving me a voice of reason and experience to lean on.

I know Serena is capable of love, just as I know she'd make an amazing mother for Violet. But if *she* doesn't believe that, if she stays locked in her beliefs that love and happiness aren't real, then the risk of her hurting me, hurting my daughter, is too high.

But the risk to my heart if I don't try? Also high.

Grabbing my phone, before I can think about it any longer, I press *call* on Serena's number. And as soon as I hear her voice, my heart settles.

"Hey, Tippy."

"Leo, hi."

She sounds sleepy, and a memory of curling up next to her in the back of my old pickup truck when we would drive out to a local park to stargaze comes back to me. Her blonde hair tickling my chin, her hand drawing lazy circles on my chest.

"Did I wake you up?"

"No, but I am in bed." She yawns. "Okay, maybe I was almost asleep."

"Well, I'd say I'm sorry for calling so late, but I'm not."

I hear the sound of her shifting around, and my mind tries not to think too hard about the fact that she's undoubtedly wearing very little clothing right now.

"Oh really," she says, her voice sounding stronger — and sultrier. "You enjoy disturbing a lady's rest?"

I let out a low chuckle. "Not any lady's, just yours."

"Hmm. What can I do for you, Leo?"

I can hear the smile in her voice. And something else. "Oh baby, that's a loaded question. You sure you're ready for the answer?"

"I wouldn't have asked if I wasn't."

Damn. I settle back in the chair, shifting slightly to ease the pressure starting to build in the front of my shorts.

"You can say you'll let me take you out on a date this Friday night."

"A date?"

God, I wish I could see her face right now so I could try to gauge her reaction. Because I don't have a clue what she's thinking. I thought I had made it clear I wanted to start something with her, but I swear I hear a thread of hesitation in her voice.

I'm pointedly ignoring the voice in the back of my head that is responsible for my own hesitation when it comes to Serena Matheson.

"To start, yeah. You, me, maybe some wine since this time we're actually legal drinking age."

"Like that stopped us before," she interrupts with a soft laugh.

"I know, I know. But this time I want to do it right, Tippy. I know I said I'd give you space to figure things out, but I also said I wanted a second chance for us. So, what do you say? Let me take you on a date."

"Okay."

Chapter Eleven

Serena

As if I don't have enough to stress about, having agreed to go on a date with Leo, I just got the utility bill for the studio, and it's bad. "Why. Why. Why." I thump my head on the barre in the studio over and over.

"Pretty sure the answer isn't to hit your head repeatedly."

I jerk up at Summer's voice, my face flaming with embarrassment that she saw me losing my shit. "Sorry. You weren't meant to see that."

She walks into the studio and comes to a stop beside me, lifting her hand to my shoulder. "What's going on? I don't know that I've ever seen you like this."

"Like what? Stressed out and going insane?" I try to laugh. "God. Just forget you saw anything. I'm a mess, but I'll be fine. What are you doing here?"

"I'm just dropping off the new yoga mat spray I made. But you're not getting out of this conversation, missy. What's wrong?"

The need to unburden everything on someone burns in my belly. With a glance to the clock on the wall, I see I still have half an hour before my next round of students should be arriving.

"Got time for some tea upstairs?"

Summer nods, and we make our way up to my apartment. I busy myself with filling the kettle and pulling down mugs while she settles on my couch. I bring over the pot of steaming jasmine tea with two mugs and sit down beside her.

"Okay. Before I tell you, can you promise to keep this a secret for now?" I ask, my eyes trained on the mugs in front of me. "I'm not exactly proud of it."

Summer's hand comes to my knee. "Of course. But Serena, I hope you know how much everyone loves you. Whatever it is, I'm sure none of our friends would judge you."

She's right. I know she is. *But they don't know how terrified I am to fail again.*

Because that's what my life has felt like. A series of failures, breakdowns, and falling apart of all the things I desperately wanted in life. And this, the studio, is my chance to keep my dream of a life in dance alive. Dance has been my one constant companion. Even with my injury and not being able to dance professionally, I've always maintained my love of movement and my passion for the grace and beauty of ballet. And if I lose the studio, I lose my last connection to this world.

But what am I doing about it? Not enough, clearly. My head has been consumed with Leo and Violet, and I haven't made any progress on figuring out my finances. Now I'm just a couple of large expenses away from having to close the studio.

"I'm broke. The studio is broke. I'm not making enough money to pay all my bills, and if I don't figure out a way to increase revenue without jacking up my class prices, I'm screwed."

"Oh, Serena," Summer murmurs.

"It's okay. I'll be fine. I can always look for a roommate." I try to make a joke, but it comes out sounding hollow.

"Have you thought of talking to Mila and Ethan? Maybe they can help somehow."

It's true, Ethan and Mila own a lot of properties in town and act as managers or landlords. But that still involves selling my studio to them and leasing the space. It still feels like a failure. "I thought about it, but... " I trail off.

"But you want to do it yourself." Summer hits it perfectly. "Serena, I know you pride yourself on your independence; it's one of the things I've always admired about you. But there's no shame in asking for help. Or at the very least, accepting it if it is offered."

I wince. "I know. It's just been hard for me to admit to myself how bad it's getting, let alone to anyone else."

"Why do you think it's happening?" she asks gently. "All of your students love you."

"They do," I admit. "But kids grow up and move on to other things, and Dogwood Cove isn't exactly a huge town. There's only so many places I can find new students. Your yoga classes help a lot, and I know I need to suck it up and offer an adult intro to dance class, but I just don't know if it'll be enough. Making my mortgage payments is getting harder as I lose students."

"Could you advertise outside of Dogwood Cove? Maybe Westport?"

"I could, but how many people will want to drive that far just for dance class?"

"It's not just a dance class," Summer chides. "It's a class with *you*. A former principal ballerina. And a wonderful teacher.

"Think I can put that on a flyer?" I quip.

"Yes. You can. And you should," she says firmly. "Seriously, don't dismiss your own appeal. A classy ad with a photo of you from when you used to perform? It'll pull people in! Throw in some reviews from current students and you're set."

"You're sweet, and I will think about it."

"Good. Now, any updates on the Leo situation?" Her eyebrows lift as she smiles, and I roll my eyes in response. But truthfully, I'm happy for the subject change.

"Maybe." I take a sip of tea, making her wait.

"Well? What!"

"He asked me out. Oh, and we've kissed a couple of times."

Summer's mouth drops open and she blinks rapidly. "And you haven't *told* us that? Good Lord, woman, you've been holding out on your best friends!" She smacks me lightly on the arm. It's meant to be joking, I'm sure, but I shift in my seat, slightly uncomfortable with her response. She's not wrong, I have been keeping it from my friends. Which isn't like me at all.

"Sorry? I don't know exactly why I didn't say anything, maybe because it's freaking me out a bit."

Summer's expression softens into one of understanding. "Ah. Anything in particular, or just the whole 'reunited with my ex-boyfriend' idea?"

"Look, I know you guys are all happy in love. And I'm thrilled for you. But how do you know it's going to last?" I stand up and start pacing, suddenly feeling twitchy and confined somehow. "From what I've seen, even the best of relationships can blow up at any moment. How is anyone supposed to trust that what they have won't disappear?"

"Serena, where's this coming from?"

I stop my pacing and study my friend for a moment. Out of everyone, she's the one person who might understand me. After all, she grew up thinking her father had abandoned her. Of course, that turned out untrue, it was her horrible mother keeping them apart, and she didn't learn that until her father died and left her a beachfront resort as an inheritance. But still, she might understand what it's like to feel abandoned by a parent, to feel like the relationship that should have been the one thing you can count on disintegrated in front of you.

"You know my parents are divorced, right?"

She nods.

"There's more to the story. See, they had what I, as a naive teenager, always figured was the perfect marriage. They held hands, talked kindly to each other, both of them came to my dance recitals, I never saw any tension or arguments. When they told me they were splitting up, it was a shock, to say the least. And neither of them would tell me what went wrong. So, naturally, I assumed it was my fault. And I assumed that all relationships were doomed to end eventually. That's why I broke up with Leo back then. We were already headed in two different directions, and even though we had talked about long-distance, I suddenly couldn't see how that would work. I thought I was doing the right thing ending it early, before we stopped loving each other."

I take a deep breath, watching Summer to make sure she's still with me. Her face is filled with compassion, so I continue.

"It gets worse. My father disappeared. I got the odd Christmas card from him the first couple of years, an email on my birthday, but nothing else. Then even that stopped. And again, Mom wouldn't tell me why. I went to ballet school without my boyfriend, without my father, and suspecting that my mother was lying to me and had been for years. I was a mess. I didn't know what to think or feel, so I defaulted to believing the only person I could trust was myself. And even that was precarious. Nothing good has ever lasted in my life. Not my parent's supposedly happy marriage, not my relationship with Leo, not my dance career, and now, not my studio."

I sink back down on the couch, exhausted from finally unloading all of my baggage.

"The concept of letting Leo in again, no matter how desperately I want to, is terrifying. For years I've believed that love won't happen for me. I'll be alone, but I'll be just fine because

I'm the only person I can trust with my heart and my happiness. Now he's trying to convince me that I've been wrong all along. And it's so tempting to give in and give love another chance, but it's also… "

"Scary as fuck?" Summer says softly.

I nod, blinking back tears.

"Oh girl, I get it. I really, really do. When I first came back to Dogwood Cove, it was really hard to let Ethan in. Despite him being all swoony lumberjack on me. But my mom's toxic nature, coupled with my belief that my dad never bothered trying to get in touch with me, messed me up. It was nearly impossible to believe this gorgeous, kind hearted, romantic man wanted me. Especially when the last time I'd seen him, he was an annoying little boy I played tag with." Summer smiles fondly, and I know she's thinking of Ethan.

"How did you get over it? What makes you believe that it's real?"

She lifts her hands in an *I don't know* kind of gesture. "There is no magic answer. I guess I just hit a point where *not* having Ethan in my life was no longer an option for my heart. I *needed* to be with him, I *needed* to love him, and I *needed* to let him love me. Sure, anything could happen in the future, but I also realized that other relationships, like my parents, don't need to have any bearing on my own. I'm not them, just like you and Leo are not your parents. Your love is not their love. Just because they didn't work out doesn't mean you won't."

"But that just feels so insubstantial. Am I wrong to want some sort of guarantee?"

"No, not wrong. Just unrealistic, maybe. There are no guarantees in life, Serena. You know this, I know this. But look at your friends. Do you believe our relationships won't last?"

"Of course not. You guys are perfect and amazing. You've all found your one true partner in life."

Summer arches her brow at my immediate response. "Okaaay, and why exactly is it so hard to believe that you deserve to find that kind of love as well?"

"I...I...I don't know," I say lamely, and it's the truth. Somehow, with all of the happiness I feel watching my friends fall in love and plan their futures, I never stopped to consider there isn't a good reason why I couldn't have that, too. Especially in light of Mom finally telling me why Dad left. It might not explain why he stayed away, but it helped to lessen the burden of thinking it was all my fault.

"Serena. It's obvious to absolutely anyone who knows you that you still have feelings for Leo, just like he clearly does for you, based on what you've told us. If he's willing to put his heart on the line, and you're willing to give things a second try, I don't see why you shouldn't." She tilts her head. "Unless — is Violet an issue for you?"

"God, no! I adore that little girl," I object immediately. "She's amazing, and he's such a great dad."

"Are you worried about stepping into a mother-ish role with her?"

"No. I mean, maybe a little? It's a big deal, I realize, dating someone with a kid, but that doesn't scare me. Giving her my heart might be easier than giving her dad my heart."

"Babe, I think you've already given them *both* your heart."

She's right. I have. Leo always had it, and Violet won me over the first time I met the little girl. Now I'm being given a second chance with the one man I've always loved and a first chance at maybe someday a family. I'd be stupid to pass it up, no matter the childhood emotional baggage I'm carrying.

"I guess I have a date to prepare for."

Chapter Twelve

Asking my cousins for help planning my date with Serena was a mistake. I got every suggestion from a simple dinner out, courtesy of Kat, to a drive to a lookout for some *privacy*, thanks to Sawyer. My head was spinning with possible plans and trying to decide which one would have the best impact. In the end, I decided on a picnic at the beach to bring back some memories from high school. We used to drive out to Haywood Lake, park my old truck backed up toward the water, climb into the bed, and cuddle under blankets watching the stars.

Hopefully, the trip down memory lane works for Serena. My goal is to get her to remember all the good times we had back then and pray it's enough to convince her our future could be just as good as our past.

Which is why I'm here on a Friday night, outside the studio, working hard to *not* overthink my plans for the evening. My hands won't stop flipping my keys around, so I shove them in my pocket and run my hands up and down my pant leg.

There's nothing to be nervous about, it's *Serena*, for fuck's sake. I know this woman. Well, I did know her.

There's a yoga class going on inside from what I can see, but the sidewalk is empty when the studio door opens, and Serena walks out, my throat thickening at the sight of her. Memories of picking her up for dates start to flood back into my mind, and I am instantly transported back twenty years. Meeting her parents for the first time, desperate to make a good impression so they would trust me with their girl, taking her to restaurants, being so proud to pay for the two of us, thanks to my job at the local grocery store, driving down back country roads with her tucked into my side.

My connection to this woman is tied up in a thousand stories, a million memories, and a lifetime of love. A love that has been given a second chance to bloom.

"You look incredible," I say, my eyes traveling hungrily over her body. She's wearing frayed jean shorts that hug her incredible ass perfectly and a sweater that drapes off one shoulder, showing a peek of a lacy bra or something underneath. Cowboy boots complete the outfit, and I do a double take when I see them. "Are those... "

"The ones you got me at the rodeo when we were seventeen? Yep." She lifts her leg and kicks it back saucily. "They still fit."

"Fuck, Tippy, you do realize you're making it really fucking hard for me right now. I'm meant to take you on a date, but all I want to do is toss you over my shoulder and carry you up those stairs. And I don't care how many people see me."

Her hazel eyes darken as they fill with lust. "Don't tempt me, Leo Talbot."

I breathe deeply, letting the exhale come out as an audible sigh that borders on a groan. "Even after all these years, you still have power over me. But I'm stronger now. I can resist your womanly wiles." I wink at her and her lighthearted giggle tells me she also remembers our senior year English teacher talking about womanly wiles during our discussion of *Pride and Prejudice*.

When we reach my truck, I hold open her door and take the opportunity to enjoy the view of her climbing in.

"No bench seat. Bummer," she says when I slide into the driver's seat a moment later.

"That's what you think," I mutter softly, then I lift up the center console, which stayed down on our drive to the Martin farm earlier this week. Serena doesn't waste a second, scooting over so that she's sitting beside me.

"Much better." Her happy smile is everything to me.

As I steer us onto the road that my cousins tell me leads to a tucked away beach about twenty minutes outside of town, I take a chance and drape my arm across the back of the seat, letting my fingers trail along her bare shoulder. When she snuggles even closer into my side, I don't bother trying to hide my satisfied smile.

"Are you going to tell me what the plan is for tonight?" She tilts her head up slightly to ask, placing one hand on my thigh, drawing circles on it with her finger.

"First of all, if you keep doing that with your finger on my leg, we're gonna be in trouble. Nobody has ever tested my self-control quite like you." I remove my arm from her shoulders and place my hand over hers instead. She instantly flips her hand over so our fingers can tangle together. "Second of all, no, I'm not." Feeling bold, I lift our entwined hands and press a featherlight kiss to the back of hers.

Serena lets her head fall to my shoulder, and we drive for a few minutes like that. The radio is on low and the woman I've always loved is beside me; it doesn't get any better than this.

Until I see her reaction at what I had my cousins help me set up down at the beach.

"Oh my God, Leo." Her gasp of surprise at the blankets and pillows set up on the sand with a picnic basket on top is exactly the reaction I hoped for.

"We can't park the truck close enough to the water like we did at Haywood, but I was hoping you still enjoyed picnics at the beach."

Serena turns toward me, her eyes shining. "I do. I definitely do. But how did you do this? How did you even know about this place?"

I shrug. "I had some help from my family. They want me to be happy in Dogwood Cove, and it's no secret that you make me happy."

Her arms wrap around my waist, and Serena tucks her head to the side, fitting perfectly under my chin like she always has. "You make me happy, too."

"That's what I was hoping you would say."

"But —" she pulls back slightly and gives me an impish grin "— I am hungry. Whatcha got in that basket?"

I laugh and lead her over to the blanket. We sit down, comfortable on pillows with nothing but the setting sun overhead and the sound of the waves hitting the shore in front of us. This really is a private location, not another person in sight. Opening the basket that Kat helped me put together with some food from the café, I pull out some containers.

"Charcuterie, a spinach salad, and a secret dessert."

"Yum," Serena sighs happily.

We eat, taking turns putting together crazy combinations from the charcuterie board, chased down with a bottle of white wine I picked up from the local winery Serena's friend Finn runs. While everything seems easy and relaxed, I can't shake the weird tension thrumming inside of me. It's as if part of me is wondering if this is real or just some elaborate dream. If you had asked me even a year ago if I ever thought I'd be with Serena Matheson again, I would have laughed if off as an impossible fantasy.

"After we split up, I used to think about what I'd do if I ever saw you again."

Serena's words startle me with how similar they are to my own train of thought. "Yeah? What were some of the options?"

She leans back on her side, her head propped in her hand. "At first, I was convinced I would run in the opposite direction. It hurt to even think of you, so the idea of seeing you after I broke both our hearts? I didn't think I could handle it. As my life went on without you, I started wishing I could see you from a distance. Just to know you were okay. But even that seemed like it would hurt so much."

I lower myself down so that I'm on my side as well, facing her. Reaching over, I tuck her hair behind her ear. "I lost count of how many times I almost called you that first year after high school."

"Why didn't you?"

"Like you said, you broke my heart. And even though I still loved you, self-preservation kept me from wanting to hurt any more than I already was. I was positive you'd move on and find some other guy, and I would be nothing but a memory."

"There was never another guy. Well, no one important, no one who meant anything close to what you mean to me."

I didn't realize how badly I needed to hear that until I do. Leaning forward, I capture her mouth in a deep kiss, trying to infuse it with forgiveness, hope, and anticipation. When Serena rolls onto her back, I follow, coming over top of her and letting some of my weight press her down into the blanket.

"I never stopped loving you," I whisper against her lips in-between kisses. Her answering moan spurs me on, and I move my lips down her neck and across the soft skin of her collarbone. My hands are holding me up so I don't crush her, but Serena has other ideas.

"Touch me, Leo. Make me *feel* again."

Lowering myself to one side of the blanket, I slowly bring one hand to her stomach, teasing her sweater up to bare her torso. I snake my fingers under the fabric of her sweater until I'm cupping her breast, stroking her lace-covered nipple.

"Oh God, yes," she moans.

I pinch and roll her nipple between my fingers, teasing it into a stiff nub before shifting over to the other side. Her hands grab my head and she smashes our mouths together in a messy, raw, passionate kiss. I'm consumed with need and desire, my cock straining against my shorts, desperate to feel her again after all this time. But it's too fast. Too soon. The tiny part of my brain that is not yet lost to lust is able to recognize that I can't rush this, it has to be at her pace. Which is why, even though I hate my fucking morals right now, I pull my hand out from underneath her sweater and drop back onto my back with a groan.

"Tippy. I didn't bring you here for this." My head shoots up at her sound of discontent. "Oh babe. Not that I don't *want this*, but I also want you. I mean, I want to date you. I mean — oh fuck." I fall back with a thud onto the blanket and close my eyes. What a great fucking time to sound like an idiot.

"Leo."

I open my eyes to the sound of her voice and see her face hovering over mine. There's no judgment or hurt in her expression, just understanding and lust.

"You're right. We don't need to rush."

Serena sits up, and I do the same. But when her hands go to the hem of her sweater and she starts to lift it over her head, I find my voice again. "I thought you said we don't need to rush?"

She tosses her sweater to the side, and it takes all of my restraint not to fall on her like a hungry dog at the sight of her with nothing but some lace covering her torso. "We aren't rushing. Do you remember what we tried to do at Haywood that one summer? But we chickened out because the water was too cold?" Her boots come off next, then Serena's tongue darts out to lick her lips as she stands up and shimmies off her shorts.

"Right now I don't remember anything," I say hoarsely, fixated on the almost naked goddess in front of me.

With a laugh, she takes off toward the water's edge. Standing there in just her bra and a barely there thong, she looks ethereal. As if she's a specter, a mirage, dancing on the edges of my sanity. When she peeks over her shoulder back at me and reaches around to unclasp her bra, my conscious mind finally catches up. I scramble to my feet, ripping my shirt over my head in one motion just in time to see her drop her panties to the ground and walk into the water.

Good. Fucking. God.

The teenage girl I was in love with, with her lithe dancer's body, is now a mature woman. She's still slender, but her curves are in all the right places, and watching her naked body enter the water has me rock-hard in an instant.

Hopping on one foot, I kick off my shoes and pull my shorts down, trying desperately not to trip in my excitement. But that excitement drops slightly when I hit the water.

"Holy shit woman, it's cold!"

Serena turns around, but she's deep enough that the water covers her incredible tits. Her eyes drop down to my dick. "From what I can see, shrinkage isn't something you need to worry about. Get in here, Talbot."

I flash her a cocky grin as I make my way out to her. "What can I say? I'm a grower *and* a shower. But you already knew that."

Coming to a stop just in front of her, I inhale deeply. "Okay, it's not so bad now that I'm in." I reach out for Serena and pull her into my arms. Her legs lift up and around my waist, bringing our bodies into perfect alignment.

"So much for not rushing," she murmurs, pressing a kiss to my wet skin.

"I'm not rushing. I'm sharing body heat."

Her indelicate snort sends both of us into fits of laughter.

"Seriously, though, can we get out now? Mission accomplished; skinny-dipping is officially checked off my nonexistent bucket list."

She grins up at me before dropping her legs down. "Yeah, fine. Let's go."

Keeping hold of her, I pivot and bend forward. "Hop on, Tippy."

Her delighted giggle has me smiling wider than I have in years. Her arms come around my neck, and I lift her up and piggyback her onto the beach, the same way I used to carry her when we were younger and being silly together. When we hit the blanket, I grab one of the spare ones and bundle Serena in it.

"You go to the truck and get it warming up while I clean all of this up."

Serena shakes her head. "No way, if we freeze, we freeze together."

Given the fact that it's late summer and not all that cold out, we aren't going to freeze. But something about this moment has connected us again. I manage to pull my boxer briefs over my wet legs and help Serena into her underwear and sweater. Then we make quick work of tidying up our picnic, scooping all the blankets and pillows into our arms, rushing back to my truck, and dumping it all in the back before climbing into the cab, breathless with laughter.

"Damn, woman. You're still wild." I turn my head to look at her. Serena is one of those people who radiates energy and joy. And right now, she's beaming.

I want her.

"Leo," she whispers.

Our lips find each other instantly. A low, feral-sounding growl escapes me as my hand cups the back of her neck, holding her to me. She's mine, now and always.

Chapter Thirteen

Serena

Climbing the steps that lead from the studio to my apartment has never felt like foreplay before. But with Leo's hand in mine, and the promise of what's coming, I'm flushed with anticipation. I hardly remember the drive home from the beach. My head is still swimming from our kisses, and the thrill of skinny-dipping is flowing through my veins.

Thankfully, Summer's yoga class is long over, and the studio is empty.

When we get inside, there's a pause. I walk over to my front window to close the drapes.

"Are you sure about this?" Leo asks, coming to stand behind me, his strong arms wrapping around my waist. "We don't have to do anything. I'm happy just being here with you."

I melt back against his chest, turning my head slightly so I can nuzzle under his chin. "Leo, I've never been more sure. This doesn't feel like rushing anything. It feels absolutely perfect."

His lips find my neck, and he sucks gently before running his tongue over the spot. "Good. Raise your arms."

I comply and he lifts my sweater off, baring my breasts to the cool evening air. I'm grateful I closed my drapes first; skinny-dipping was enough public nudity for one night. His hands cup my breasts, finding my nipples and teasing them into stiff peaks.

"God, your body only got sexier. You drive me crazy, Serena."

"Mmm," I moan as he continues to kiss my shoulders, my neck, anywhere his lips can reach. I slide my hands back around his neck, arching my spine, pressing my breasts into his hands. "Leo...more... "

"I'll give you more. Be patient."

His gruff voice is new, as is the dominating way he's handling me and speaking to me. And holy guacamole, do I love it. I know my sweet and caring Leo is still here, and I'm completely safe. But the darker, sexier, grittier side of this older version of him? Yes, please.

"Stay just like this, Tippy," he growls into my ear before catching my earlobe in his teeth. His hands disappear for a moment, but then he's back and his naked torso is pressed against my back, a wall of heat behind me.

I bite back another moan.

"Let me hear you."

Leo's hands are back, sliding to the front of my underwear, the last thing I'm wearing. He pushes them down, and I use my legs to help get them to the floor and kick them away. His fingers immediately zero in on the center of me, stroking gently, up and down, tantalizing and torturing me.

"Touch me, Leo. Please," I pant.

"Shh. I'm in charge right now. Just trust me. Can you do that?"

For a split second, I freeze at his question. And I know Leo feels it.

"Hey, babe. Serena, what happened?" He withdraws his hands and goes to spin me around, but I hold him in place.

"Nothing. I'm sorry." Tilting my head up so he can see the truth on my face, I continue, "Trusting you. That was never a question. I've always trusted *you*, it's me I don't trust. Or I guess, it's love. But never you."

There's a second or two of silence before Leo's head drops down to my shoulder, and his arms tighten around me even more. "Serena, if you trust me, then trust *my* love. It's never stopped, even after twenty years, and it never will. And no matter how long it takes to help you believe in our love and in yourself, I'm here. Every step of the way. Because I won't go through losing you again."

I draw in a shaky breath, blowing it out slowly. Then I say the only thing that's right in this moment.

"I love you."

I turn around in his arms and pull his head down to meet mine. Our lips collide, and it's a new beginning. A layer of my pain and confusion has fallen away, and I feel lighter.

Leo lifts me up into his arms, turning us away from the window.

When we reach my bedroom, Leo lowers me to the bed, then steps back and looks around. "I see you still haven't caught the housekeeping bug."

My head whips around to see where he's looking, and mortification floods my cheeks. I jump up, swipe the dirty bra and socks off the ground, and dump them in my hamper.

"I didn't exactly know we'd come back here, okay?"

He laughs as he walks up behind me and once again captures me in a tight squeeze. "It's fine, Tippy. Not the first time I've seen your bra on the floor of a bedroom, and it won't be the last if I have anything to say about it. I'm just teasing you, babe."

I roll my eyes, thankful he can't see me.

"I know you're rolling your eyes at me. You forget, I know you better than you know yourself."

"Seriously?" I cry in outrage, smacking at his hand that is splayed across my naked stomach. "Enough about my laundry. Why are you still wearing clothes?"

"Because I want to finish what I started earlier."

His talented fingers zero in on my wet sex, sliding between my legs easily. He runs the pad of his thumb in a light circle over my clit and my body bows from the sensation. The entire evening has been a game of slowly building foreplay, and I am beyond ready for the main event.

"I want to touch you," I say breathily, but Leo just chuckles, and I feel his head shake against my neck where he's kissing me.

"Not yet. First I need to reacquaint myself with something."

"Wha-?" I gasp as he plunges his fingers inside of me, curling around and finding my G-spot immediately. It's a skill that took him a month to master when we were younger, and clearly, he hasn't forgotten a thing.

"Oh my God, Leo. Shit. Yes," I mumble, my hands gripping his forearms as I writhe around, desperate for the release that I can feel teasing me, just out of reach.

Proving just how in sync he is with me, Leo withdraws his fingers, ignoring my cry, only to pivot me and push me back onto the bed. I scramble to raise up on my elbows just in time to see him drop to his knees, and then his tongue is on me, licking my slit all the way from my ass to the very tip of my clit.

"Fucking hell, Tippy. You taste even better than I remember."

The vibration from his words against my sensitized skin has me dropping back, my hands finding his hair and tunneling in to hold him in place.

Leo's hands come to my legs, and he throws them over his shoulders, grabbing my hips and pulling me in even closer. How he's breathing, I don't know, and I don't care. All I care about is the thousand sensations coursing through me as he plunges his tongue in and out of me, bringing one hand back to my clit, alternately pinching and circling it.

"Oh God. Yes, yes, yes, yes! Right there. Ohmygod. Don't stop," I moan, my body starting to convulse.

"Leo! Leo! Oh shit, Leo!" I scream as my orgasm overwhelms me, catapulting me to the stars and back with waves of pleasure over and over again. This is twenty years of missed Leo-induced orgasms all at once. I don't realize just how intense it is until I drift back to reality and discover Leo is stretched out on the bed beside me, one hand resting on my stomach, and his lips are gently kissing away tears that are leaking from my eyes.

"You better be crying tears of joy, or I'm going to need to up my game."

I let out a shaky laugh. "If you up your game anymore, I'm gonna die of orgasm."

I feel his lips turned up in a smile when Leo moves to kiss my mouth.

"I'll just bring you back to life with another one."

"And so the cycle continues? Die by orgasm, revive by orgasm? Something's wrong with that plan," I say impishly.

Leo falls onto his back with a laugh. "Goddamnit woman, you're ridiculous. Complaining about orgasms. What's next?"

It's my turn to prop up on my elbow. "Hey, who's complaining? I'm just saying it seems inefficient, the whole dying and reviving portion of this. Can't we just skip that and keep the orgasms?"

"Deal."

My breath catches at the look I see on Leo's face. It's one I haven't seen in a very long time. It's a look that promises he's mine, and I'm his.

I shift so that I'm on top of him, my naked body straddling his half-clothed one. "We need to deal with this," I say, bringing my hands to the top of his shorts. Together we make quick work of removing them and then, at last, I have his dick in my hands.

It may sound weird to describe a cock as beautiful, but Leo's truly is. Long, thick — but not too thick — with a perfect, smooth head. I wrap my hand around it and slowly stroke up and down, earning a rumble from Leo.

"Yeah, Tippy. Fucking hell." He lets out a loud exhale as I twist my hand at the top and slide back down. Lowering my head, but keeping my eyes trained on his face, I lick him from root to tip, slowly, before taking him in my mouth. My tongue swirls around his cock, and I let the salty, musky taste of him fill my senses. Giving head is the ultimate power trip for a woman, and I fucking love it.

Bobbing my head up and down, I alternate sucking and licking, letting my hand follow with the same twisting and squeezing motion. I remember what Leo likes, what gets him harder than granite, and sure enough, mere minutes later, he's pushing me off of him.

"Goddamnit woman, you are way too fucking good at that." He flips me over and looms over me, my hands coming to grip his powerful forearms. His lips find mine, and our tastes mingle together. It's a passionate and deeply drugging kiss. One that makes you lose all sense of time and space.

But one part of my body is still aware of things, aware enough, at least, to feel the tip of his cock sliding through the wetness between my legs. I lift my knees and wrap my legs around him, locking my feet just above his ass.

"I need you, Leo. All of you. I'm on birth control and safe if you are."

He nods and that's enough of an answer for me. I trust him.

"You've got me, Tippy."

With one thrust, he fills me as I cry out his name again. We both pause for a second, our foreheads touching, our breathing in sync, and we adjust to this incredible feeling of being connected in the deepest physical way possible once again.

"I need to move," he whispers, and all I can do is nod. Leo slides almost all the way out of me, then back in, slowly this time, achingly slow.

"More," I moan.

He pulls out again, and this time, he slams back in. One hand finds my ass and grips it hard, pulling me in to meet his thrust every time. We settle into a rhythm, Leo's movements both familiar, yet new and exciting. My body responds the way it always has, with a steady build of the inferno inside of me.

All of a sudden, Leo pulls out, then manhandles me as if I'm nothing more than a rag doll, flipping me onto my stomach, grabbing my hips and lifting them in the air, then slamming back inside.

"Oh fuck, yes," I shriek as his hand comes down to lightly smack my ass right before he grabs my flesh and squeezes it in his hands with a grunt. I never knew I was into this type of borderline rough, definitely dirty sex, but apparently, with Leo,

I am. My back arches, my spine curving naturally, thanks to years and years of dance training.

"Fuck yes, babe. You're perfect. God, Serena. I fucking love you." He grunts out the words as he slams into my body.

When he lowers himself over my back and snakes one hand underneath me to find my clit once again, my hands give out on me, and I collapse onto my chest on the bed. Clutching the pillow as he pushes into me over and over, his hand teasing my clit, pinching and rolling it as I cross the point of no return, letting my release crash into me like a tsunami, wave upon wave of intense pleasure.

Even in my euphoric state, I still sense when Leo finally lets go. I can feel his release filling me and hear his voice hoarsely crying out my name.

And in the immediate afterglow, with our bodies tangled together on the mess of my sheets, I finally feel complete and at peace for the first time in twenty years.

CHAPTER FOURTEEN

"I think it's safe to say our sexual compatibility is still there," I say once my breathing returns to normal.

Serena turns her head and giggles into my chest. "You are *such* a nerd."

"But I'm right, aren't I? I'm pretty sure that was two orgasms for you, missy. I would've gone for three, but you seduced me with your smokin' hot body and I got distracted."

Her hand lightly smacks me. "Good grief Leo, deflate the ego a bit, would you?"

I capture her hand in mine, lifting it to my mouth so I can kiss it. "Do I want to know when you decided you liked a little spanking?"

"Umm, let's see. It was... "

I lurch my body up and over her and kiss her lips to stop her from answering. "I don't really want to talk about the guys you've been with, Tippy. Not while we're naked."

She pushes against me firmly. "Would you let me finish? I was going to say it was about fifteen minutes ago, you big jealous idiot."

I drop my head down to her shoulder with a chuckle. "Oh." My lips find the curve of her neck and I trail kisses up to her ear, letting my teeth graze her skin, feeling her shiver in response. "The way your body responds to me is so fucking hot. I forgot how fun your flexibility can be."

Serena's moan has me hardening again — already. Jesus Christ. Knowing Violet is happy at Aunt Claire's house for the night should make it easy for me to want to stay right here, throw her long legs over my shoulders, and dive back into Serena's luscious body. As if she's reading my mind, Serena shifts underneath me.

"When do you have to pick up Violet?" she murmurs, pressing her soft lips onto my chest.

"Umm, later?"

"Seriously?" She picks up her head, lifting her eyebrows at me, confused. "What exactly does later mean?"

"It means my brain is scrambled by the sexy naked woman lying on top of me."

Her giggle has me grinning in response.

"Huh. Okay, I guess that naked woman better back off then so you can think straight." She goes to lift off of me, but my hands hold her firmly in place.

"First, you forgot sexy. Second, you're not going anywhere. I don't need to think straight for —" I glance over at the clock on her wall "— at least another hour."

"In that case… "

There's a wicked glint in her eyes that promises dirty things. Even so, I'm not ready for the feel of her mouth around my cock. It has me closing my eyes with a groan as I'm surrounded by her wet heat.

"Hell, Tippy. You are a goddamn goddess."

Her hands join her mouth and she starts to work me over. My hands tangle in her hair, taking hold and guiding her movements. I freeze at the sound of her choking on my dick, but this fucking insane woman only looks up, covers my hand with hers, and pushes her own head down.

"You sure?" I ask hoarsely.

Her answering moan reverberates around my dick. Jesus Christ. Somewhere in the last twenty years, Serena developed a naughty streak. And as long as I don't stop to think about how that happened or what other man is responsible, I can let myself just enjoy it.

Her tongue swirls around the tip of my cock, her teeth grazing along the underside lightly. Then she takes me fully in again and slides one hand down to stroke the overly sensitized skin beneath my balls.

"Fuck," I say on a long, low groan. With that one movement, she destroys any control I might have had over my body's reactions.

"Serena, I'm gonna come."

She speeds up slightly, one hand twisting and sliding in perfect tandem with her mouth, sucking, swirling, licking, driving me crazy.

"Oh shit. Yes. Yes, babe. Yes. Fuck, yes!" I come with a shout, and my incredible woman drinks me down, not letting up until, with a shudder, I pull back, lifting her off of me. I drag her up my body, gently pushing her hair away from her face.

Her tongue darts out to lick her lips and I can't help but kiss her. Even the taste of myself on her lips doesn't bother me; I'm too consumed by Serena.

"Mmm. That was fun." She licks her lips, giving me a wicked smile.

"Glad you enjoyed it," I joke. "Meanwhile, I'm ruined. You just destroyed me with that gorgeous mouth of yours."

Serena lifts her shoulder, and her hair falls forward. "If you think I'm going to apologize, you're wrong."

"It's not an apology I'm after."

"No? Then what?"

"A promise."

Her light laugh makes her tits jiggle perfectly. "A promise of what?"

"That later, after I ruin *you* in the shower, you'll remember the feel of my mouth on you for the rest of the night."

Even with getting very little sleep last night, this morning, I'm energized.

"C'mon kiddo, let's go get breakfast with Auntie Kat before I go to work." I clap my hands together and Violet comes tripping down the hall, her hair flying behind her. She's got a giant smile on her face, and it brings one onto mine as well.

She's happy here.

"Daddy, I haf cootee, pease?"

"Nice talking, Vi! But you need to eat some breakfast first, then we can talk about a cookie. Okay?"

Man, when did she start using almost complete sentences? She's growing up so damn fast.

Vi skips over to the front door and plops down on the floor. God, I got so lucky with her. She might be shy with new people, but other than that, she's such an easygoing, happy kid.

I crank the music on her favourite Disney playlist for the short drive into town and park at the police station. The walk over to Camille's café isn't far, and a part of me is hoping to see Serena.

Pushing open the door to the café, Violet's hand clutches mine tightly. There are quite a few people in here, but when she sees my cousin, she starts pulling me in that direction.

"Auntie Kat! Auntie Kat!"

"Hey, peanut!"

Kat walks over and drops down, arms open, and I watch my daughter beeline for a hug. She and Kat are becoming close, and it's a huge relief to have another adult with whom Violet has connected.

When I reach the two of them, Violet is babbling on to Kat about who knows what, but my cousin is nodding and smiling as if she follows every word.

"Come on, missy, let's sit down and get breakfast before Daddy has to go to work." I lift Violet up and sit her down at a nearby table. "Can you grab her some milk, Kat?"

My cousin nods. "You betcha. Coffee for you?"

"Yes, please. And a breakfast sandwich." I ruffle Violet's hair. "Hey Vi, what do you want today, eggs or pancakes?" Yeah, it's a trick question. I already know the answer.

"Pancakes, pease."

Kat gives us a thumbs up and heads over to the counter to put in our order as I reach into Violet's backpack to dig out a hair elastic.

"We forgot to braid your hair, honey, you okay with a ponytail today?"

"Rena!"

My head snaps round, searching for her. Vi starts squirming in her seat and I let her go. Serena's over on the bakery side of the building, but she must hear Violet because she turns around just in time for Violet to crash into her legs, squeezing them.

I make my way over, my hands stuffed in my pockets so I don't do anything stupid like hug her just as hard as my daughter.

"Hey," I say softly over Violet's head.

"Hi."

"Sleep well?"

I see her fighting back a smile as a flush covers her cheeks. "Yeah. I did. You?"

Slowly I shake my head. "Not really. Couldn't stop thinking about last night."

I don't miss the catch of her breath and wink at her.

"Hey you two, breakfast is ready over here."

I twist over my shoulder to wave at Kat before facing Serena again. "Would you like to join us for a bit?"

Please say yes...

"Sure."

We wind our way back to our table, and my hand manages to find the small of Serena's back in a way that is perfectly acceptable. No matter how much I want to claim her in public, we haven't talked about that yet. And I haven't told Violet that Serena is more to me than just her dance teacher. Two things I need to fix, ASAP.

"Hey Serena, can I get you anything to eat?" Kat asks once we're sitting down. I'm busy cutting up Violet's pancakes as she works on her milk mustache.

"No, thank you, I was actually just grabbing some tea and a muffin next door." Serena holds up a bag and a to-go cup. "I've got to get ready for class soon."

"Me dance?" Violet goes to wipe her face on her arm and I catch her just in time, using a napkin instead.

"Yes sweetie, it's your dance class this morning. I can't wait to see you twirl."

"Braid like Rena, Daddy?"

It takes a minute for my brain to disengage from memories of last night that are definitely not okay to be thinking about around my three-year-old. When I do, I can't figure out what she's asking.

"What's that, Vi?"

"You want your hair braided like mine, Violet?" Serena stands up, putting her hand on my shoulder. "I got this, Daddy."

Hearing her call me daddy, even in this context, is way fucking hotter than I expected. I start to count backwards from twenty to try and contain my physical reaction.

"Do you have a hairbrush here?"

I lift Violet's bag, letting the back of my hand run up Serena's leg as I do. It's subtle, the touch hidden by our bodies, but she doesn't miss it. Guaran-fucking-teed she stood close enough to me on purpose, and I'll take any opportunity to feel her skin against mine.

"Thanks."

If I'm not mistaken, there's a breathy note to her voice that definitely wasn't there before. Mission accomplished.

I eat my breakfast and help Violet eat hers while Serena's hands fly over Vi's head, twisting her hair into a way more complex braid than what I could have done. The entire time, my eyes are bouncing between the daughter I love more than life itself, and the woman who has always owned my heart.

I want this. Shit, do I ever want this to be my life.

"There you go, missy." Serena sinks down gracefully into her chair and takes a sip of her tea.

"What do you say, Violet?"

"Fank 'oo," Vi says around a mouthful of pancake.

"You are so welcome. I better go and get ready for class." Serena stands again just as Aunt Claire walks up.

"Well, look at this, what a wonderful breakfast you're all having."

I don't miss the innuendo in her words and give my aunt a pointed stare that hopefully tells her to let it go. "Hi, Aunt Claire. We're just finishing, then Vi is all yours. Can I get you a coffee?"

"Oh no, I'm fine." Aunt Claire bends down to press a kiss to Violet's head. "Your hair is so pretty Vi, did Daddy do that?"

"Rena do it."

If her eyebrows could go any higher, they'd be off her face. "Really?"

"Oh, it's nothing. I just quickly braided it while she was eating," Serena says hurriedly. She's blushing, and it's making me want to pull her into my arms even more. Just so everyone knows she's with us. Like, really with us.

"It's lovely." Claire puts a soft hand on Serena's arm, and I see Serena relax visibly. "Oh, Leo, I'm so sorry, but I won't be able to stay with the little miss on Sunday. I completely forgot Dennis and I have plans to meet friends in Victoria for the day. Do you think the chief will let you switch your shift?"

Shit. Serena really did ruin me last night; I completely forgot I'm meant to attend a workshop in Westport on Sunday as part of my conditions of employment. The workshop is part of a program aimed at building leadership skills, and Chief basically said it was a requirement for me to complete it as a new deputy chief. It won't look good to cancel so last minute, but hopefully the chief is understanding.

"Ah, no. It isn't a regular shift. But I'll cancel." I pull out my phone to send an email requesting a meeting with the chief.

"I'm so sorry, honey," Aunt Claire twists her hands together and I can see she's about to give up her plans for me.

That's the last thing I want. If anyone is sacrificing something for my kid, it's me.

"Don't worry about it, Aunt Claire. She's my kid, my responsibility. I'll figure it out."

"Leo, I can spend the day with her."

I look up at Serena, who's fidgeting with her tea, looking at me nervously, as if she expects me to refuse. The truth is, I'm staggered that she's offering.

"Really, Tippy? It's a full-day workshop, and I have to drive to Westport and back. I'll be gone the entire day."

She lifts her shoulders and gives me a cautious smile. "We'll have fun. If Violet is okay with spending the day with me, of course."

"Vi, what do you think, are you okay staying with Serena on Sunday?"

Violet's head doesn't even lift from her plate of pancakes. "Otay, Daddy."

"Well, okay then," I say with a smile at my little girl. I shift my attention back to Serena and my aunt.

Aunt Claire looks relieved. "Thank you, Serena. And I am sorry, Leo, it completely left my mind when I said I could help."

"It's fine." The words are directed at my aunt, but my eyes are fixed on Serena. "Serena, can I walk you to the studio?"

At her nod, I stand up, kissing Violet's head. "See you tonight, kiddo."

Once we're outside, my hand finds Serena's lower back again as we head down the street the block or so to her studio. I don't say a word and neither does she until the door is open and we're inside, away from prying eyes. Only then do I cup her face gently, and at last, kiss her.

"That's how I wanted to say good morning to you," I murmur against her lips, feeling them tip up in response. I kiss her again, deeper this time. "And that's to say thank you for saving my ass this Sunday."

Serena tilts her head to the side and twists around to look behind me. Her hands squeeze the globes of my butt tightly as she smirks at me. "Well, you know, I kinda like you, so… "

"Jesus Christ, woman," I groan, letting my head drop to meet hers. We kiss, and kiss, and kiss some more. I lose any sense of time and place, captivated by her mouth.

Her hands slide around my waist, pausing when she reaches my handcuffs. Drawing back slightly, Serena's eyes flash down to the cuffs, then back up to me, an unreadable expression in her eyes.

"Have you ever, umm, used these with someone?"

My eyebrows raise up to my fucking forehead. "Are we talking while I'm on duty or off?"

"Off duty." Her pupils dilate. "Definitely off duty."

"No," I reply hoarsely. "Never had a woman I wanted to use them with. Why? Do you want me to cuff you, baby?"

Serena draws in a deep, ragged breath. "I...I don't know. I've never trusted anyone enough to give them that kind of control."

Fuck. Me. I want to earn that trust. I want her to give herself to me. But only when she's ready.

The alarm on my phone goes off, warning me of my upcoming meetings and shutting down any opportunity to talk about this further. But make no mistake, I want to talk about it. Because I don't think I'll get the mental image of Serena cuffed to my bed out of my head anytime soon.

Chapter Fifteen

Serena

"She's only a kid. You spend time with kids all day long. This is going to be fine. *You* are going to be fine."

My pep talk monologue is doing nothing to calm the butterflies in my stomach. There's a huge difference between teaching a class of twelve for an hour and spending an entire day with one child. One very special child whose father just happens to be the man I've been in love with my entire adult life.

I pull into Leo's driveway a few minutes early and just sit in my car, staring at his house. It's cute. Perfect for a small family, and I can see evidence of Violet everywhere, from the chalk scribbles on the driveway to the abandoned toys in the front yard.

"Come on, Serena. You like Violet. Heck, you probably love that kid more than any other. You've got a plan, and worst case scenario, you take her to the farm to play with Layla and the animals." I run through my list of activities one more time. I don't think we'll make it out to Abby and Reid's farm, but it's a good backup if I need it.

A knock on my window makes me shriek in surprise.

"Sorry, babe, I thought you saw me." Leo is laughing as he helps me out of my car and kisses me softly.

I don't think I'll ever get over the sight of him in uniform. I mean, he's always sexy, whether he's in shorts and a T-shirt, pajamas, or nothing at all. But Leo in full police uniform? That makes my panties wetter than anything.

Maybe it's seeing him living his dream, maybe it's the confidence in himself and his career, or heck, maybe it's just the innate sex appeal of a man in uniform.

"How long were you watching me talk to myself like a crazy person?"

"Long enough to know you're *my* crazy person."

He kisses me again, long and slow, and I feel any worry or stress about today melt away under his touch. It's always been this way. He's the calm to my storm. He says I fill him with joy and energy, I say he balances me out with a deep, peaceful stillness.

"Violet's just eating breakfast. She's really excited to spend the day with you."

I tilt my head back so I can look at him, and the look shining in his eyes melts me even further. I didn't realize I could love this man more than I did when we were younger, but I do.

And that's both terrifying and exhilarating at the same time.

"Good. I'm excited, too. You wrote out her routine, right? I remember she sometimes naps in the afternoon, but what time? Oh, and allergies, she doesn't have any, does she?"

My brain starts firing at top speed again as soon as we begin to walk up toward the house, and Leo tugs me to a stop at the bottom of the steps to his front porch.

"Tippy, calm down, babe. She's an easy kid, I promise. No allergies, no weird sensitivities. She might nap, she might not, but she slept well last night, so she'll be okay either way. You can stay here and play, go to the park, the beach, wherever. I've set out extra clothes, her bathing suit, sunscreen, and anything else I could think of. There's snacks and lunch ready in the fridge, and she's hoping to convince you to order pizza for dinner. She likes ham on it, but no pineapple." Leo counts off on his fingers as he lists everything he's prepared, and my eyes widen further and further.

"Wow. You did all of that already? I didn't even remember half of that stuff."

He chuckles. "I'm her dad, babe. It's my job to remember all of that."

The sense of overwhelm I've managed to squash down threatens to rear up again. *He's a dad.* And I'm just...a dance teacher.

No. I'm a damn good dance teacher, and a good person. Leo trusts me with his little girl, and we're going to have fun.

There, that's the pep talk I needed.

"Alright, let's do this." I march up his steps, Leo jogging up behind me. I can still hear him laughing to himself, but I don't really care that he knows I'm nervous.

"Rena!"

Violet's happy shriek comes from the direction of what I'm guessing is the kitchen, and I head down a short hall that way. Sure enough, she's strapped in a booster chair at the table, scooping what looks like oatmeal into her mouth. Half of it drips off the spoon and back into the bowl, a bunch more gets smeared on her face, and I guess some of it actually ends up in her mouth.

"Welcome to the first step in spending a day with my daughter," Leo murmurs in my ear. "Trying not to laugh at how much food she gets on her face versus how much she actually eats."

His fingers stroke up and down my spine and I shiver at the contact. It's delicious and slightly naughty, seeing as his oblivious toddler is right in front of us. I lean back into his hand and turn my head slightly to whisper back at him, "Note to self, no soup for lunch."

Leo snorts under his breath, then to my dismay, he steps away. I immediately miss his nearness, but watching him say goodbye to Violet is pretty much the cutest thing ever.

"Be good, baby girl. I'll be home later tonight, okay? Rena is going to spend the whole day with you, and when she says it's bath time, you listen. Got it?"

"Otay, Daddy. Rena baf." Vi nods solemnly. It's hard to not laugh, what with the oatmeal covering her cheeks, but somehow I manage.

Together Leo and I walk to the front door where he picks up a black leather satchel. Turning to me, he runs a finger down my cheek before kissing me softly.

"Fair warning, Tippy. She might say she'll take a bath now, but when the time comes, be prepared for a fight."

I mime pushing up my sleeves. "I can handle it."

He studies me for a moment, his eyes warm on mine. "You know I love you, right?"

I nod, unsure where he's going with this.

"Good. Remember that when my daughter turns into a hellion and drives you nuts later today."

My laughter follows him out the door, and his grinning face is the last thing I see as he pulls out of the driveway, leaving me alone with his precious girl.

It's go time.

After breakfast is done and Violet is cleaned up, I let her lead me into her bedroom. My heart squeezes at the photos on her dresser, of Leo holding a tiny baby, looking down at her with absolute amazement in his eyes. There's one of a woman, too; I'm guessing this is Alexa. It says a lot for Leo's kind heart that he keeps a photo of the woman who abandoned her daughter, although it also makes me wonder how he'll handle the inevitable questions when Violet gets older.

Violet shows me all of her favourite toys, then pulls out a book that is clearly well loved. The pages are bent, and Vi makes a show of sounding out her own version of the words. She points at the pictures of all the animals and makes the appropriate noises. It's freaking adorable and gives me a fantastic idea of what to do next.

"Do you like to read books, Vi?"

The way her eyes light up as she gives me an emphatic nod tells me exactly what I suspected. I think Paige has a kindred spirit in Violet.

"My friend Paige has a bookstore. Should we go and visit her?"

"Yes, pease!"

"I love your manners. Okay, let's get you dressed and then we'll go."

It takes a lot longer and a lot more energy than I expected to get a three year old dressed and out the door, so by the time we're parking on Main Street in front of the bookstore, I'm exhausted.

I think I can understand why so many parents survive on caffeine.

Pushing open the purple door, I hear the familiar jingle of the bells Paige installed. I had texted her before we left Leo's house, so my best friend knows to expect us.

"Hello." Paige appears in front of us with a light smile on her face as she looks down at Vi.

Falling in love with Wyatt softened Paige's stiff and formal exterior. Don't get me wrong, I've always loved her, even when she was way more reserved. But now she's much more relaxed and open. Violet really does remind me of her in so many ways; they're both shy and slow to warm up to new people, but once they get to know you, they show the beautiful heart and soul they have inside.

"Violet, this my best friend Paige. She loves books just as much as you do." I crouch down beside Vi, but she's gone shy, turning and burying her head in my shoulder.

"Up, Rena."

"Oh, okay." Standing, I lift her into my arms carefully. I've never held her, or any kid for that matter, not even our friend Riley's new baby. And I know it's because I'm the only option right now, but still, having Violet turn to me for security and comfort makes my heart swell.

"Can you say hi to Paige? Or do you want to just go and look at some books first?"

"Books."

I give an apologetic shrug of my shoulders to Paige, but she obviously empathizes with Violet.

"I'll be up front reorganizing some shelves, why don't you choose a few to take to the chairs and read?"

"Thanks, Paige." I shoot her a grateful grin and carry Violet toward the back of the store where the children's books are, then set her down. "Alright kiddo, why don't you choose two books for us to start with?"

I have to hold back a giggle at how big and round Violet's eyes are as she takes in all of the books, as well as the brightly coloured cushions and decorations that Paige set up in the children's corner of the store. One wall has a mural of animals all over it, and Vi heads straight to it, her hand reaching out to touch the monkey swinging from a vine.

"You really like animals, don't you kiddo?"

"Amals?" She turns to me. "Rena read amals?"

"You want me to read a book about animals? Okay, let's find one together."

An hour later, we finally left Pages with two books that Violet chose. As we were walking out, Vi surprised both me and Paige by waving at her and even saying a quiet "fank you" without me telling her to.

From there it was off to the elementary school for a snack and some time on the playground. I keep expecting Violet to get tired, but if anything, she just has more energy as the day goes on. Maybe she's siphoning it from me because I'm thinking I could use a nap right about now. How parents of more than one kid handle it, I don't know. How Leo has done it as a single parent, I *really* don't know.

When we finally make it back to my car, which we left outside the bookstore, Violet points at the sign for The Nutty Muffin.

"Tweat?"

"Can we get a treat?" I shrug. Leo never said we couldn't, but I don't exactly know the protocol on kids and treats. Still, today is a special Serena and Violet day. "Sure, why not. Let's go. Maybe we'll choose something for Daddy, too."

It takes Violet an adorably long time to choose a treat for Leo, but only seconds to pick out her favourite cookie.

By the time we make it back to their house, it's midafternoon. I rummage through Leo's cabinets while Violet sits on the floor with her cookie, and when I come across a box of my favourite peppermint tea, I send a mental thank you to Leo for being so thoughtful.

"Alright, what are we going to do now?" I ask, settling down on the floor next to Vi, my tea safely up on the table.

"Read." Violet thrusts one of her new books out at me, and I take it with a laugh.

"We already read this one three times at the store. You want to hear it again?"

"Read." She nods. "Pease."

"Well, okay, since you asked so nicely. Let's go sit on the couch and read."

My phone vibrates in my bag as we stand up to go to the living room, and I pull it out to check, my mouth turning up when I read the message.

LEO: How are my two favourite girls doing?

Glancing up to make sure Violet's okay, I quickly type out a response.

SERENA: Her energy is insane. But we're good.

And because I can't resist messing with him, I send another message

SERENA: One question though. You're okay with having bunnies right? Because we might have stopped at a pet store...

LEO: What? Seriously?

SERENA: Okay no, I'm joking.

SERENA: They're guinea pigs not rabbits.

LEO: Tippy...

LEO: Stop messing with me. Did you really get my kid guinea pigs?

SERENA: Omg. You're still so gullible. No. I did not get her any animals

SERENA: Except in book form.

LEO: I'm confused.

I walk into the living room and sit beside Violet, holding up one of her books while she's looking at the other. "Hey Vi, smile for a picture for Daddy."

I snap a quick selfie of us and send it to Leo.

SERENA: See? Animal books. I assume those are fine.

LEO: Jesus. You're not good for my blood pressure. Yes books are fine.

LEO: I love you.

SERENA: Love you too. Now go away. We have guinea pigs to read about.

LEO: See you later babe.

"Serena, babe."

My eyes blink open slowly at the sound of Leo's warm voice and the feel of his hand stroking my arm. I'm crammed into Violet's tiny toddler bed where I must have fallen asleep with her when I put her to bed.

"Hi, you're home," I say, stating the obvious. In my defense, I'm a little groggy. But I manage to get out of the bed and follow Leo into his kitchen. That's when I realize he's not in uniform anymore, oh no. All he's wearing are low-slung pajama pants that are showing off way too much of his delicious and shirtless body.

"No fair."

"What?" He raises one eyebrow quizzically.

"You look yummy. And I can't stay."

His quiet laugh shouldn't be sexy, but then again, everything Leo does is sexy.

"Am I supposed to apologize for wearing pajamas?"

I shake my head slowly. "No, but could you maybe not wear them so... " My voice trails off as I wave my hands up and down. "So delicious-looking."

"I'm wearing pajamas in a delicious-looking way? How can clothing even be delicious? It's not like you eat it." He's teasing me and I narrow my eyes at him. Two can play at this game.

"It's not the clothes that are delicious. It's what's *underneath* the clothes."

Leo groans, exactly as I hoped he would.

"Exactly," I huff, crossing my arms. "And now I have to leave, and it's not fair."

Leo prowls over to me, gathering my hair up in his hands and bending down to kiss my neck. "Why do you have to go?"

A moan escapes me, and for a second I forget why I need to leave. I mean, I guess I could stay.

"I...I don't have clothes. Or a toothbrush."

"You don't need clothes. And I have spare toothbrushes."

"Work."

"We can get up early."

"Umm. Gah." I lose my train of thought completely when his hand tugs my shirt down, exposing my nipple, and he covers it with his warm mouth.

"Wait. Wait, wait, wait, wait." I push him away, gasping at the sensation of his lips popping off my breast. "Are we really ready for Violet to wake up and find me here?"

Leo steps back, running his hands through his own hair and letting out a loud sigh. "Damn it. I wish you weren't so adorably responsible right now."

I slap his bare chest lightly. "I've been responsible all day, thank you very much."

He pulls me back into his arms, but gentler this time. "Yeah, you have. And have I told you how much I appreciate that or how amazing I think you are?"

I tilt my head to one side. "I mean, yes, but you can always say it again."

"You're amazing." Leo kisses my forehead. "And I appreciate you hanging with Vi today." He kisses my nose. "And I love you." This time when he kisses my lips, it's soft and sweet, and although I still want to get naked and stay the night, I know we've both realized that we're not there yet.

"I'm gonna talk to Vi about you. Tell her you're more than just Daddy's friend or her dance teacher. Because I want you to spend the night. I want to wake up with you in my arms. I want everything with you."

I shiver as his words reverberate in my heart.

"I want that, too."

CHAPTER SIXTEEN

Leo

It's been two days since Serena spent the day with Violet, and my daughter has not stopped talking about it. They connected in a way I don't even fully comprehend. All I know is my little girl has never been happier and more confident. She smiled at the cashier at the grocery store instead of burying her head in my shoulder and even whispered her thanks when they offered her a sticker.

Somehow, Serena's worked her magic and is drawing Vi out of her shell, and the change is incredible. The fact that other people are getting to see the happy, cheerful little girl I know Vi can be is everything to me.

I pick Serena up tonight to take her for dinner at a restaurant in Westport that was recommended to me by one of the guys at work. Aunt Claire has Violet for a sleepover for the first time, and I'm equal parts nervous to be away from my daughter for so long and excited to have an entire night with Serena.

I almost canceled, thanks to my little girl being extra clingy and fussy all day. I'm guessing it's because she's nervous about spending the night away from home, and while I know everything is going to be fine, I feel guilty leaving her when she's unhappy.

But it's not hard to refocus my attention on Serena as soon as I pick her up. Her long legs are on display under a flowy yellow dress. Hell, I barely remember taking her for dinner. I'm sure the food was good, but I was too distracted by Serena's feet under the table, sliding up and down my leg, tantalizing me, tormenting me, and winding me up faster and harder than I've ever been.

Every bite she takes, I swear she turns sexual. With little noises, coy glances, subtle touches, every instant of the evening is torturous foreplay.

When we get back to Dogwood Cove, we both run up the stairs to her apartment, tripping and laughing in anticipation. I know she wants me just as badly as I want her. The door slams shut behind us and I spin her around, lifting her into my arms and pushing her against it.

"Mmm, Jesus, babe, you've been driving me crazy all fucking night. I can't wait to get you in my mouth," I growl against her neck, biting down just hard enough to make her gasp before sweeping my tongue over the spot to soothe it. I want to mark her, show the world she's mine now that she's agreed to go public, but even I'm not that much of a caveman.

"Leo," she whispers, her hands fluttering in my hair. "Leo." I register the fact that now she's pushing against me and I abruptly set her down and step back, panting.

"What? What's wrong?"

"Nothing," Serena purrs, lifting her short dress up and over her head, revealing her perfect tits to me. "There were just too many clothes between us."

"Fuck, yes," I breathe, pulling my shirt off as well, just in time to catch Serena as she jumps back into my arms. The lace covering her breasts scratches my chest lightly and keeping one hand firmly on her hip, I move the other up to unclasp her bra. She leans back just enough to pull it off and fling it over my shoulder as I turn us, still kissing her, and make my way to the couch. I sink down, keeping her in my lap, and kiss her, letting it turn messy and chaotic, frenzied with arousal.

The searing heat between us never wavers as our tongues dance together, lips seeking contact over and over again. I move down the smooth slope of her neck, finding the hollow at the base where it meets her shoulders, swirling in a circle, letting her moans and sighs guide me. Not that I need it; I've had her body memorized for twenty years.

Somehow we move, twisting slightly so that I'm lying down, stretched out on her couch, and she's over me, her hair falling in a curtain around us and our legs tangled together.

The slide of her body over mine is pure heaven. She starts to grind her hips down over my already hard cock, and I move to lift her up, intent on moving us to the bedroom.

But the ring of my phone breaks the moment. Briefly, I consider ignoring it, and I know the battle of what to do is playing out on my face by Serena's response.

"You need to answer it. What if it's about Vi or work?"

As I sit up and look for my shorts on the floor, with my phone ringing in the pocket, I look over my shoulder and fix her with my stare. "Let's get one thing straight. Work will never come before you and Violet."

Her face melts into a dreamy, lovestruck expression, and I mentally fist pump. Until I see the display on my phone. A missed call from Aunt Claire and a text.

AUNT CLAIRE: Leo, I'm sorry to interrupt your evening but Violet has a fever. I'm perfectly fine managing it on my own, but she keeps asking for you.

"Shit." I thumb out a reply, only vaguely aware of Serena getting off the couch and walking over to me.

LEO: I'll be there as soon as I can.

I drop my phone on the coffee table and grab my shorts. "I'm sorry, Tippy. I have to go. Vi's sick with a fever."

"Oh no," Serena says, and the protective papa instinct in me wants to lash out at the disappointment in her voice until she carries on, "I hope she's not feeling too terrible. Give her a big hug from me, and let me know if you need anything tomorrow, okay?" She presses her lips to my shoulder and I spin around, pulling her into my arms and crushing her body to mine.

"Thank you."

"For what?"

"For being you, for loving me, for understanding."

"Oh, Leo."

The expression on her face just about brings me to my knees. It's so beautifully laced with love and compassion.

"I love you *and* your little girl. Now go, be with her." Serena kisses me firmly, then pushes me toward the door.

How I got lucky enough to have a second chance with this woman is beyond me, but I swear, I'll live my entire life showing her how much I love her.

Right after I take care of my baby.

I push open the door to my aunt's house without knocking, trying to stay quiet in case Vi is asleep.

"Daddy?" comes a sad and tired-sounding voice, and Aunt Claire walks out of the living room with Violet tucked up in her arms.

"Hi, baby girl," I whisper, taking her from my aunt, and wince at the heat radiating off her. "I hear you don't feel so good."

I press a kiss to the top of my daughter's head and shoot my aunt a grateful smile.

"She had some medicine and some juice, but I think she just needed her daddy's magic to feel better," Aunt Claire murmurs. "I'm sorry to interrupt your evening."

I shake my head. "It's fine. Vi needed me."

"I know, but you needed —"

"It's fine," I interrupt firmly. "Vi comes first. She was acting kind of off earlier today, so I'm not that surprised she's sick. Honestly, I never should've gone out in the first place."

"Leo." Placing her hands on her hips, my aunt glares at me. "You going out tonight did not make her sick, so don't you dare let yourself feel guilty for this in any way at all."

Letting out a sigh, but not bothering to deny what she said, I turn away. Instead, I start looking around the room to locate any of Vi's belongings that I need to take home.

"Leo, look at me." At the no-nonsense tone in her voice, I reluctantly look over at Aunt Claire. "You're an amazing father, selfless and giving. You always put Violet first, and she will forever know you love her."

I open my mouth to interrupt, but she holds up her hand to stop me.

"And you're a man. Not just a father. If Violet never sees you doing things for yourself, focusing on your own happiness, how will she ever know to value that for herself? Do you want your daughter growing up never knowing that her own happiness is just as important as the happiness of her loved ones?"

Well, shit. When she puts it that way...

"Of course not." I let my head tip back to the ceiling, close my eyes, and try to breathe out some of the stress, worry, and guilt coursing through me. "Thank you. And thanks for calling me."

Seeming satisfied with my response, Aunt Claire turns, picking up Violet's bag that I hadn't even realized was at her feet, already packed, and hands it to me. "I'll call you in the morning to check in, but don't hesitate to text me if you need anything. No matter the time."

"I will, I promise." With one last wave, I carry my daughter and her stuff out to the truck. Violet whimpers when I set her in her car seat, shooting an arrow through my heart. There's truly nothing worse than your kid being sick and feeling almost helpless to do anything.

Still, as I drive the short distance between my aunt's house and mine, I do my best to remember what she said and not let the guilt overtake me.

It's hard not to.

Because the reality is, while I was getting it on with Serena, my little girl was suffering without me. She was sick, and I was about to have sex.

When we get home, Violet is, thankfully, asleep. I manage to transfer her from the car seat into her bed without her waking up, a small blessing, probably due to the medicine giving her some relief.

By the time I get into my own bed, it's midnight. But I can't sleep. When I close my eyes, I'm bombarded by flashes of memories from earlier with Serena. The smell, taste, and feel of her. Both new and familiar at the same time. The sounds we both made, the love I swear I saw in her eyes.

I had envisioned bringing her tea in bed in the morning, then waking her up with my tongue and fingers. We'd make breakfast together, and maybe head back to bed once again before I'd leave to go back to my daughter.

Instead, my life smacked me in the face and told me to get my priorities straight.

The knock at my door the next morning is an unwelcome interruption. Violet was up at three and again at six this morning. She's cranky, I'm tired, and even though her fever isn't as high as it was last night, it's still higher than I would like it to be. At least right now she's napping.

I open the door, fully prepared to bark at whoever it is, but Serena's the last person I expected to see.

"Not a good time, Tippy. I'm sorry about last night, but Vi's really not feeling great," I say tiredly. My body aches to pull her into my arms and steal whatever peace I can from her, but I also know that after a night of cuddling a very sick little girl, chances are I probably caught whatever Violet has, and I don't want to make Serena sick.

"I'm not here for an apology, I'm just here to drop off a few things." Serena whips out a mask from her back pocket and puts it on. "And no offense, but I'm not gonna kiss you."

She pushes past me and heads straight to the kitchen. Only then do I realize she's carrying two grocery bags.

I follow and find her unpacking cartons of juice, Violet's favourite apple sauce pouches, some fruit juice popsicles, granola bars, my favourite coffee already ground, what looks like soup from Camille's café, and a box with The Nutty Muffin logo on it.

"I wasn't sure what you both felt like eating or drinking, so I tried to get a variety of easy stuff. Especially for the little miss. When I was googling 'fevers in children' this morning, it said keeping them hydrated was the most important thing. So I figured juice or apple sauce would be our best bet. I also picked up another bottle of fever-reducing medicine in case you were out and some lemon scented bubble bath. The internet said sitting a kid in a warm, but not hot, bath can also help them feel better."

I take Serena by the shoulders and spin her around to face me. "You researched how to treat a fever?" I say, my voice full of amazement. Serena blushes and stares at the floor until I tip her chin up.

"Well, yeah. When you left last night, I was worried about you both. I want to help, but I really can't afford to get sick. I don't have anyone else who can teach my classes. I figured bringing you some supplies would be the least I could do."

"God, I really want to kiss you right now," I mutter, tempering the growl with a smile. "You're amazing, you know that?"

Her blush intensifies. "It's just some juice and muffins."

"No, Tippy, it's more than that. It's you caring about me, about my daughter, enough to take the time to figure out what would be helpful and then doing it. Your capacity for love is endless. And witnessing that energy directed toward Violet is more than I ever expected. I just... I'm... " I huff out a sigh. "Thank you."

Violet chooses that moment to cry out for me from her room.

"Shit, I better go check on her. Can you stay for a minute?"

Serena shakes her head, "No. Sorry, I have to go to the studio and start preparing some advertising stuff." She starts to back out of the kitchen and I can sense her goddamn walls going up again. I just don't know why.

Violet calls out my name again, her little voice sounding extra pitiful and stabbing me with guilt that I'm not instantly running to her side. But I can't shake the nagging suspicion that Serena's about to bolt. And not just in a physical sense.

"Serena," I start toward her but she lifts her hand up.

"Your daughter needs you, Leo. I'll talk to you later."

Helpless to stop her, I watch Serena walk out of my house. There's no way for me to go after her and demand she tell me why she's retreating right now. Not while Vi is waiting for me.

Being a father may be an incredible blessing, and my daughter is the light of my life.

But right now, not only do I feel like I failed Violet by leaving her last night, I'm also failing myself — and Serena — by letting her go.

Except there's nothing I can do about that. All I can do is remember my number one priority.

My daughter.

CHAPTER SEVENTEEN

Serena

"Your capacity for love is endless... "

I've rolled those words around in my head all day, distracted from the things I was meant to be doing as I tried to make sense of it.

"Serena, seriously?" Ashley claps her hands in front of my face, snapping me out of my inner thoughts. "Look, if this isn't a good time then let's meet later."

Shit, she sounds annoyed. "I'm sorry, Ash," I mumble, dropping my head into my hands as I slump forward in my chair.

"What's wrong?" she asks, her tone softer now. I lift my head off my desk.

"It's Leo. Well, no, it's me. I'm so freaking confused." When Ashley doesn't say anything, I sit up straighter. "Do you think second chances are good?"

Understanding dawns in her eyes. "I mean, sometimes, yes. In a way, Finn and I needed to give each other a second chance."

I consider that for a moment, and she's right. Sort of. "But is it different when there's so much time and life between things? You and Finn, or any of the others, your second chances were about immediate forgiveness of stupid choices and miscommunications. With me and Leo, our second chance is about relearning each other, falling in love all over again, and trying to forgive everything that happened. Except there's twenty years of life separating our past from our present."

"Right, but why did you have twenty years apart?"

Oh.

"Stupid choices and miscommunications."

Ashley nods her head as if she's just solved world peace. "Exactly. The only difference is time. And maybe you guys needed all that time to get to a place in your lives where you could actually work through those mistakes and come out stronger and better for each other in the end."

"You're really smart, you know that?"

Ashley grins at me, then folds her arms across her chest and leans back in her chair. "I do, actually. That's also why you asked me to help you figure out marketing your new adult intro to dance class, remember?"

"Yeah, yeah." I chuckle, and we turn our attention back to the ad mock-ups we've been working on. "Okay, let's do this. If I have to torture myself teaching grown-ups, we might as well make me sound good."

After Ashley leaves, as I get ready for my after-school classes, I think about Ashley's comment. There's no denying that Leo and I have grown and matured over the years. But was that a good thing for our relationship or not? My heart and my gut says it's a good thing. Which means I need to stop running from my feelings and stop avoiding the hard stuff I need to do in my life.

Easier said than done... Enter Exhibit A — my reluctance to teach adult classes despite *knowing* it's the obvious solution to my income nightmare. Even if it means more late nights teaching since I can't exactly do them during the day.

But today seems to be the day for wake-up calls, courtesy of Ashley. Her help and encouragement have me sending the ad off to the Dogwood Cove and Westport newspapers, as well as posting it online. Also, her insight makes me realize I want to check in on Leo. And probably apologize for rushing out on him this morning.

I could see how conflicted he was when I went to leave, torn between his absolute need to be there for Vi and his desire to talk to me. But his daughter needed him, and I needed some space. Because the reality of being with a man who has a child started to dawn on me in that moment.

SERENA: Hey, how's Vi?

LEO: Her fever broke thank god. And she's loving the juice pops you brought over, thank you.

SERENA: Good. And how are you??

LEO: Tired. Wishing our night hadn't been interrupted. I'm so sorry about that.

Shit. I read his message over and over, analyzing every word to death. This is exactly what I'm afraid of. That our relationship will never work because I'll come between him and Violet somehow. And no matter how much he tries to have us both, that's impossible. His guilt will eat him alive, and he'll have to choose. And, of course, he'll choose her. He has to choose her.

But where does that leave me?

I thumb out a reply in a daze, processing the overwhelming sense of dread building in my stomach.

SERENA: Don't apologize, she needed you.

LEO: I know.

LEO: I just feel bad that I had to leave you.

Every alarm bell that surrounds my defensive heart is going off. My brain starts running a million miles an hour, envisioning how this could play out.

This won't be the last time Leo has to be there for Violet. Her needs will always come first, as they should. I mean, Leo's dedication to his kid is one of the most attractive things about him. He's always been a natural caretaker, a nurturer, and a giver through and through.

And that parental instinct and dedication mean I come second.

Which puts me *first* in line for being left. Abandoned. Rejected.

I knew this was too good to be true. I knew Leo and his incredible daughter were not for me. Because the pain of eventually losing them both will destroy me.

SERENA: It's okay.

SERENA: I gotta go, I'll check in later.

I toss my phone into my bag, turning it to silent so I'm not tempted to read any reply he might send.

The roller coaster I've been on mentally and emotionally today has me feeling utterly drained, and it's not even lunch time.

When I walk into my accountant's office that afternoon and come face to face with Beckett Donnelly, I'm paralyzed. My feelings are still too raw from earlier; if he asks me anything about Leo and me, or our relationship — whatever that means — I don't think I can answer.

"Hi Serena." He walks up to me with a warm smile. Distractedly, I analyze his face. Now that I know they're related, I can see a lot of similarities between him and Leo. How did I not see it before?

"Beckett, hi," I reply awkwardly, twisting my hands. *Where's Henry?* For once, my usually punctual accountant is late, damn it. And on the day that I *really* don't want to make awkward small talk with Leo's cousin.

"I heard Violet isn't feeling well, have you talked to Leo?"

"Yeah, I, uh, I dropped off some food and stuff there this morning."

"Oh, great. That was nice of you." Beckett slides his hands into his pockets and tilts his head to the side. "It's funny, we've all been living in the same town for so long and had no clue of our mutual connection. Fate works in mysterious ways, huh?"

All I can do is nod dumbly.

"Anyway, I won't keep you. But you should know my mom is bugging Leo to bring you to a family dinner soon. You'll be up against the full force of the Donnellys."

I swallow nervously. "That sounds lovely," I manage to say.

Thank God, Henry finally decides to make an appearance at that very moment.

"Ah, hello, Serena. Sorry to keep you waiting." Henry gestures down the hall to his office, and I follow him, turning over my shoulder at the last second.

"Bye, Beckett. Nice to see you." There, that wasn't too awkward, was it?

I push any anxieties over Beckett or Leo out of my brain as soon I sit down opposite Henry and take in his serious expression and steepled fingers.

"Serena, you've been my client since you opened the studio," he begins and my stomach sinks. "I've watched you grow your business, and I've seen how much effort and energy you put into it and into this community. But —"

Oh God, here it comes.

"The concerns we've discussed about your declining enrollment and the increasing costs of running the studio are only getting worse. I ran the numbers for the next quarter, and it's not looking good, to be frank. We need to figure out an immediate plan of action to bring in more money. Especially since we can't adjust your mortgage payments anymore."

"I'm increasing the number of yoga classes, and I recently started advertising for an adult dance class." My response sounds feeble at best, and we both know it. A couple more classes isn't going to be enough.

The rising interest rates, coupled with the increase in the cost to simply run the studio, as well as my slowly declining enrollment as kids grow up or stop taking class for any number of reasons, have put me in a really tight financial position. The writing has been on the wall for a while now, but I've avoided facing it.

"That's a start, but as much as I hate to be the bearer of bad news, it won't be enough. You've already deferred two mortgage payments, the bank won't let you do a third. Without a significant influx of cash flow to cover expenses and make up those payments, the bank may choose to take action."

"And that means?" I ask, my voice barely above a whisper.

"That means you risk foreclosure." Henry's words are harsh but stated calmly. I know he doesn't mean anything by them, it's simply the truth.

"Now, obviously, we don't want to get to that point. And I know you've worked hard to prevent this from happening; we both have. We made all the right moves and decisions we could, but they haven't been enough." He pauses, leaning forward on his forearms and giving me a sympathetic look. "My recommendation at this point is to consider an investor. Someone who can purchase the studio, take over the mortgage, and then rent the space out to you for your use."

It's the easiest solution, but also the one I really don't want to consider. "I'll think about it."

And I will. Right after I finish thinking about Leo, and my dad, and Violet, and the adult dance classes I'll be teaching, and the million other things occupying and causing chaos in my mind at the moment.

Later that night, after Summer's yoga class at the studio, I find myself sitting with my friends on the comfortable chairs of Mila's bakery. Even though The Nutty Muffin is closed, we all decided cookies were needed, so here we are.

"Did you send off those ads?" Ashley asks as she sits down beside me and hands over a cup of chamomile tea.

I blow on the hot liquid and nod. "Yeah, bring on the grown-ups who want to live out their childhood dream of being a ballerina."

Ashley snorts at the sarcasm dripping from my words. "It can't be *that* bad teaching adults, can it?"

My pointed stare gets the point across perfectly clear.

"Why are you doing it if you hate it that much?" Mila calls out from the kitchen, where she emerges carrying a tray of goodies. I grab a brownie from the top, hoping someone else will say something to help me avoid the question.

But no one does.

Instead, they all look at me, waiting for my answer.

And weirdly enough, I find I want to tell them. I'm tired of carrying it all by myself. And there's a difference between telling them all my problem and expecting them to fix it.

"The studio is losing money. If I can't find more students or teach more classes, I won't make my mortgage payments and I'll have to sell."

Everyone looks shocked. Only Summer had any idea of my situation, and she's looking at me with nothing but compassion.

"But it'll be fine. I'll figure it out, don't worry." I hurry to fill the stunned silence. "The adult classes will help."

"Will that be enough?" Mila asks, getting straight to the point of things. I can't lie, so I shake my head.

"I'll think of something."

"Why didn't you tell us earlier?" Paige says, and I turn to her, guilt written all over my face. Out of anyone, she's who I should have talked to sooner. She's my best friend and a fellow business owner, not to mention one of the smartest people I know. If anyone could have helped, it's Paige.

"Honestly, I don't know. I was embarrassed? I didn't want to admit to anyone, not even myself, that it was getting so bad."

Showing a rare display of physical affection, Paige leans in and gives me a hug. "But we're your friends, and we care about you. Supporting you, helping you stave off financial ruin, is our responsibility."

"Well, when you put it that way," I joke, tears clouding my eyes. "I'm sorry, guys. I just didn't know what to say."

"What you say is, 'I'll never keep something like this from you again,'" Mila says firmly. "And you say, 'I know I'm not alone, my friends are the best women on this planet, I will trust them and be open to them from here on out.' There's no such thing as TMI within our group, whether it's about sex, men, our bodies, or our jobs. We're not just friends, we're family. And family is there for each other. Got it?"

I stand up and yank her in for a hug. Other arms join in, and soon I'm surrounded by the women that give me strength, friendship, and love every single day.

"Thank you."

Later, when I'm walking back to my apartment, I pull my phone out of my bag, only to see a text from my mom asking me to call her. I guess I never did get back to her after hanging up on her a couple of weeks ago. I'm feeling good after talking to my friends, so if there's ever a time to hear what she has to say, I guess now is it.

Once I'm home, I change into my pajamas and crawl into bed before calling her.

"Hey Mom."

"Hi, sweetie." She sounds cautious, worried even.

"Sorry I haven't called you back sooner, it's been busy."

"That's fine. I understand. Can I…talk to you about your dad?"

Mentally, I try to prepare myself for whatever she's going to say. "Yeah. I guess so."

"Okay. Now, before I repeat what I told him I would say, I want you to promise to listen to me and not freak out." She pauses, and I realize she's waiting for me.

"Fine, I won't freak out until I hear what you have to tell me. Is that good enough?"

"I could do without the snarky tone, but yes." My eyes roll at her words. *Too bad, Mom. You're getting snark.*

"He wants to talk to you."

I snort, but before I can reply, Mom continues, "He actually said he wanted to see you in person, but I convinced him to start with a phone call. I know you haven't heard much from him since he left, and I know I probably screwed up by never telling you what happened, but you're an adult now. So I'm hoping you can understand when I say there was more to it than what we told you back then."

"More? You told me nothing!" I shout, sitting up in bed. "Nothing, Mom. You told me you and Dad were getting a divorce and that you hoped with me going away to dance school it would make it easier for us all to adjust. *That* is all you told me."

"It wasn't my story to tell," she says quietly and I pause. She sounds defeated.

"I need to know, at least something, if you want me to consider talking to him again."

"Your dad... " She stops, and I hear her take in a deep breath. "Your dad had a gambling problem. A bad one. And it eventually destroyed our marriage and our future. If he hadn't left to go to rehab when he did, you wouldn't have had any money left for dance school."

I'm stunned. Of all the things, I never imagined this.

"But my dance money, that was in a trust."

"It was, and your dad was searching for the paperwork to break the trust and take the money to pay off his debts when I caught him. You were out with Leo that night, but when you came home, you were so excited, talking about your future, that your dad finally realized he was ruining our lives. He chose to go, but I chose to end the marriage. I just couldn't take it anymore."

We both fall silent for a few minutes.

"Why does he want to see me now?" I whisper when I find the ability to speak.

Mom sighs. "That's also technically his story to tell, honey. But I will say this. I only want what is best for you, and I truly think talking to your father is what's best. He needs this, but more importantly, I think *you* need this to heal. I gave him your number, Serena. Please just...just talk to him if he calls."

When we eventually hang up, I immediately head downstairs. An hour of freestyle dancing does little to clear the madness in my head; there's simply too much going on in my life right now. Even the usual peace and serenity that dance brings me is eluding me.

But it does at least make me tired enough to fathom the idea of going to bed. And in the cover of darkness, I force myself to face the fact that Mom might be right. I do need some closure from my father.

Doesn't mean I'm looking forward to it, however.

Chapter Eighteen

Leo

LEO: Good morning babe. Miss you.

This is the third day in a row I've messaged Serena as soon as I wake up. And the third day in a row she hasn't answered.

Okay, that's not entirely true. Yesterday she sent one back, several hours later, that said good morning.

I don't want to push her or seem desperate or clingy, but she's pulling back, I know it. I had a sinking suspicion something like this would happen that morning Violet was sick and Serena came by with groceries and supplies for us. Her big heart wouldn't let her stay away, but I could sense those walls were back up around her heart. I had clearly taken one step forward and two steps back.

"Rena!" Violet's excited little voice catches me off guard. We're out for a walk on a trail my cousins said was easy enough for me to take her on. Apparently, if you keep going, there's some hot springs, but I don't think we'll make it that far. She convinced me to carry her on my shoulders pretty damn quickly.

I could feel her twisting and squirming but didn't realize it was because she saw someone behind us.

I stop and spin around carefully. Sure enough, there's the woman who has been haunting my thoughts for even longer than the last few days coming up behind us, dressed in a tank top and some sexy little shorts. She's breathing heavily and a gleam of perspiration covers her face. She's the epitome of girl-next-door perfection. Except for the look of trepidation on her face that I wish I could erase. I hate knowing she's nervous or upset about something. Even more so when she won't let me in so I can try to fix it.

"Fancy meeting you here," I call out, forcing a positive tone to my voice so my empathic daughter doesn't pick up on anything.

"Hi, you two," she answers, giving Violet a warm smile before flashing me a more cautious look. "I was just out for a run. Are you enjoying your walk?"

"I didn't know you ran."

Her eyes flash defiantly. "Guess you don't quite know everything about me anymore."

A heated moment passes between us until my daughter breaks it.

"Down, Daddy!"

I lift her off my shoulders and she makes her way right over to Serena, then lifts her arms.

"Up, Rena."

Serena hides her smile and puts her hands on her hips. "Excuse me, missy, how do you ask nicely?"

"Up, pease."

It's my turn to fight back a grin. Serena's managed to form a really amazing connection with my daughter, but that's not a surprise to me. Watching her lift Vi up into her arms and the easy way Vi settles in also comes as no surprise. Serena might not realize it, but she's a natural with children, and not just as a dance teacher. She's loving and generous with her praise and affection, but not afraid to set boundaries and expectations. She'll make a hell of a mom someday.

And yes, I want her to be that with me.

With Violet.

A vision of the three of us as a family is clear as a bell to me. Violet calling Serena 'Mommy,' the three of us together all the time. Having a partner in this madness known as parenthood, Violet having a mother, and me having Tippy by my side.

It's everything I want, now and always.

And right here, right now, I decide my mission is to make Serena see that future as hers for the taking.

"Can we convince you to change your run into a walk?"

It's not really a question; I don't think my daughter will let Serena go now that she's got her. But still, when she nods in agreement, I let out a mental sigh of relief. Things have been so off these past few days that I don't think I really knew how she'd handle this.

"How far up the trail are you planning on going?"

I lift my shoulders. "As far as the little miss can handle."

"Did you bring your bathing suits?"

"Nah. I doubt we'll go all the way to the hot springs."

The play of emotions across her face is intriguing. In the end, she looks to Violet, then back at me, and I can sense some sort of inner decision has been reached. I just don't know what that is.

"Did you know about the secret pool that's just a little bit farther from here?"

"No... "

"What do you think, Vi, want to get your feet wet?"

Violet nods enthusiastically, and Serena turns back to me. "It's shallow and warm. And a great spot to take a break, but only a few people know about it. Do you trust me?"

"Of course I do."

But do you trust me?

Funny how that word keeps coming up between us. Trust. Five letters that have the power to change the course of our stories, both past and present.

Serena's smile is quick but solid. One brick down, a few hundred to go before that wall around her heart is dismantled — hopefully, for good this time.

We carry on the trail a short while before Serena must see some landmark because she veers off to the side, pushing some branches apart to reveal a different, smaller trail.

I help Violet over some roots, but my kid is a trooper, thanks to plenty of weekends hiking and walking on the North Shore Mountains over on the mainland.

"We're almost there," Serena calls over her shoulder. The sunlight hits her, lighting her hair up so that it gleams like strands of gold. It steals my breath for a second. She's so fucking gorgeous, and she's here. With me. That reality is so unbelievable it almost chokes me up. I never anticipated this happening in a million years, but here I am.

And here we are.

Serena comes to a stop and I let out a low whistle. "You weren't kidding, this place is incredible."

Appearing out of nothing is a small pool cut into the rocks. The light smell of sulphur is the telltale sign that it's part of the hot springs, but other than that, it's paradise. The green canopy of the forest around us is full of life and colour, the sun filtering through the trees casting its warm glow everywhere. Birds are chirping somewhere, but otherwise, it's silent. Pure, natural, peaceful beauty.

But even this stunning setting can't compare with Serena. She pivots on her feet in a slow circle, stretching her arms overhead, revealing a sliver of tanned skin across her stomach.

Fucking hell, a part of me wishes Violet weren't here so I didn't have to hide my reaction. As it is, I turn sideways and try to be subtle about adjusting myself, or at least the part of myself I don't have much control over around Serena.

But when I look back, Serena's grinning at me, and I know she's fully aware of her affect on me. I widen my eyes at her, then slowly wink when her tongue darts out to moisten her perfect bow-shaped lips.

"O-okay, well, I'm gonna get my feet wet," she says chirpily, her face a beautiful shade of pink. Whatever weird shit is going on in her head right now, at least I can still turn her on.

I busy myself helping Violet take her shoes off, then she takes Serena's outstretched hand. It amazes me how easily and completely I trust Serena with my daughter. As if she was always meant to be here with us.

It's full circle to the feelings I had back in high school when I wholeheartedly believed Serena was my end game, my forever love.

"Come on, Miss Vi, want to feel how warm the water is?"

Violet's delighted giggles mingle with Serena's throaty laughter as they splash in the water. The scene unfolding in front of me has me frozen, wishing I could capture this moment in time and hold onto it for eternity.

"Are you joining us?"

I blink rapidly, shocked to feel moisture pooling in the corner of my eyes. Only Serena Matheson is capable of turning me into just as much of a sentimental sap as my own daughter.

Just over an hour later, the three of us are sitting on the shore, having splashed in the water and eaten a snack. Violet's head is in my lap, and I can tell by her slow, easy breaths that she's asleep.

"I wanted to thank you again for bringing all those treats and stuff that day Violet got sick."

"It's fine. Really."

Damn it, gone is the soft and easy energy that had finally come back between us this morning. I should have kept my mouth shut and not brought up that day. Judging by the way Serena's entire body has stiffened and the fact that she's shifted slightly away from me, I was right in thinking she was avoiding me this week.

"What happened, Tippy? Just now. And last week. Why are you pulling away?"

The words fall out of me before I can stop them. I don't mean it to sound accusatory, but the flash of hurt on Serena's face tells me she feels differently.

"Sorry. I didn't —"

"No. Don't apologize. I… God, what are we doing, Leo?"

Well, that's not the response I was expecting.

"Now? Or in general?" I ask, not really sure I want to hear her answer.

Her laugh is harsh and cuts through the peaceful afternoon, leaving a jagged, painful opening.

"Both? I don't know. You have a daughter, Leo. A daughter. Someone who needs you more than anyone or anything else. And I have a business that needs me. Can we really do this? Can we really give ourselves to each other when we're torn in so many different directions?"

My mouth falls open as I try to unpack everything she's just said. "What does your dance studio have to do with anything when it comes to us?" Maybe that's not the right place to start, but it seems the easiest.

I see indecision warring on her face, and the realization stings that she doesn't know if she can open up to me about whatever it is.

"I might have to sell the studio."

I can sense that's a massive revelation from her, but I still feel incredibly stupid because I can't connect the dots.

"And?"

Serena leaps to her feet. "And? And that studio is my life. My dream. The only one I have left that I haven't destroyed somehow. And now I'm going to lose it, just like I lost everything else."

Carefully shifting Violet onto the blanket underneath me, I stand and take Serena's hands, leading her a short distance away. "Slow down, babe. What the hell do you mean?"

Serena sags underneath my hands. "I'm losing money. I don't have enough students or classes to pay my bills."

I choose my words carefully. "Okay. We'll come back to that in a second, I promise. But I want to talk about you thinking you've lost everything, or destroyed it, or whatever that insanity was."

A sob escapes her as her arms come across her body and I watch the beautiful woman I love fold in on herself, crumpling under the weight of her emotions.

"Isn't it obvious? Anything good in my life has never lasted. My family, my career, my relationships, and now my studio. What's the common denominator, Leo?"

Jesus fucking Christ. "You seriously think all of that was your fault?"

Is this what's holding her back? What's making her pull away from me? Some fucked-up notion that she can't have happiness in her life?

"Your parents' divorce was not your fault. Your ballet injury was not your fault."

"I disagree because I'm the common denominator. Besides, me leaving you? My studio failing? That *is* on me, Leo. The two things that I've ever loved the most in life, I lost." She's openly crying now, her hands slamming down on my chest over and over. I take the hits, letting her get it all out.

"Oh, baby." I stop her flailing hands with my own and crush her into my body. "Baby, you haven't lost me. I'm right here and I love you. I always have."

"But you're not mine anymore." She sounds so broken and defeated, and I'm at a loss over how to fix this.

"What do you mean I'm not yours? My heart has always belonged to you, Serena Matheson. And only you."

"Not anymore. Now it's hers." Serena points to my peacefully sleeping daughter and something in my heart turns over. "Your heart belongs to your daughter. As it should. But where does that leave me? Because eventually, you'll have to choose. Something will happen, like when she got sick, and you'll choose her. You have to choose her. A parent should always choose their child." The crack in her voice is a dagger straight to my heart, but that's nothing compared to how I feel when she continues.

"And I won't survive losing you again. Not now. Not now that I love you both."

To say I'm stunned is a fucking understatement. I never realized the depth of damage her parents' divorce did to her until this very moment. But before I can even open my mouth to respond, Serena pivots away from me and hurries back over to the blanket, frantically throwing her things into her backpack.

"Wait. Don't go," I whisper yell, trying not to wake Violet. "We need to talk about this."

"I can't Leo, I can't talk about it. Not right now. Please, just give me some time."

I grab her arms. "Don't leave me, Serena. You don't want to lose me, well, the feeling's mutual. I can't lose you again, so please don't leave."

Finally her eyes meet mine, and the mixture of love and anguish in them kills me.

"I...I'm not leaving you. Not like before. I just need to breathe, to focus on the studio."

"What about us?" I demand, not willing to let her leave without some sort of guarantee this isn't history repeating itself with Serena running from me before some imaginary thing can drive us apart.

"I don't know."

Suddenly, I'm filled with anger. Not directed at Serena, but at the younger version of myself who let her walk away the first time. Who allowed these feelings of defeat and failure to fester inside of her, making her who she is today — someone who, apparently, doesn't think she deserves love or to be loved.

"My heart is big enough and full of enough love — more than enough — for you and Violet. It's different now, sure. But you are no less important to me just because I have a kid. If anything, watching you with her makes you *more* important because you mean something, not just to me, but also to her. So don't run away, Tippy. Please. I'll give you some time, but what you and I have is not going anywhere. Not ever again."

She nods, licking her lips.

"Promise me. Promise me you won't run."

There's a beat of painful silence.

"I promise I won't run. But Leo, how do I know there's truly enough room for me in your life and you won't abandon me? How do I trust that?"

"By trusting *me*. You said you did that night in your apartment. Did you mean it?"

"I...I...I don't know. Yes? I don't know anything right now." Her breath catches on a sob, and I yank her into my arms.

"I'll wait for you to figure it out, Tippy. For you to find your way to the truth, which is us. This." I gesture back to Violet. "The three of us. Vi and I will be waiting for you to be ready."

But as I watch her walk away, I can't help but wonder if I just lied to her.

What if she never figures it out? What if she never realizes I'm here for her and that our love is real? Can I wait forever for something that might never happen?

On the other hand, how can I not?

My foot kicks a nearby rock in frustration. Then another. The only thing that keeps me from taking all of my anger out on whatever I can find is the knowledge that my little girl is asleep nearby.

It always comes back to Violet.

Which is exactly what Serena is worried about.

And I don't have a goddamn clue what to do about it.

"Hey, baby girl, you like Rena, right?" I tuck the blankets closely around Violet, stroking back some hair from her face.

She gives me a sleepy nod. "Mm-hmm."

I've thought about how to make this clear for a three year old, and now it's time to give it my best shot.

"Daddy likes Rena, too. What if she came over here more, maybe had sleepovers and breakfast with us. What if we went out the three of us a bunch more. Would you like that?"

Violet's eyes widen. "Yes!"

I can't hold back my smile. "That's good, kiddo. I want that, too. Maybe we can ask her tomorrow if she wants to have dinner with us this weekend."

"Otay, Daddy." Her eyes are drooping as I lean down and give her a soft kiss, then tiptoe out of her room.

Grabbing a glass of water, I head out onto the back deck and pick up my phone to call the one person I'm hoping can shed some light on this mess.

"Hi, honey."

"Hi, Mom."

"To what do I owe the pleasure of a late-night phone call from my favourite son?"

I let out a low chuckle at that long-standing joke. "I'm your only son, Mom."

"That doesn't make you any less my favourite. Now, talk to me. I can hear the pain and confusion in your voice from across the country."

Inhaling deeply, I let it all out in one long breath. "Do you remember Serena Matheson?"

"Of course, I do," she chides gently. "How could I forget the first girl you ever loved?"

"She's here."

There's a second of stunned silence. "In Dogwood Cove?"

"Yup. She teaches dance. She teaches Vi, actually."

"Wow. Leo, honey. How...how are you?"

My mother knows exactly how destroyed I was when Serena broke it off with me. With it being just the two of us for most of my childhood, not to mention the incredible loss we shared, we had a closer relationship than I imagine most kids have with their mom. When she wasn't sick with grief, she was the best mom I could have hoped for. We talked about everything.

"I'm fine. Actually, I was better than fine. God, Mom, she's still so beautiful, so amazing. And Violet loves her."

"And so do you."

"Yeah," I say on a sigh. "Yeah, I do."

"Oh, Leo." I can hear her worry even over all the distance between us. I stand up and walk back into the kitchen, intent on grabbing a beer. Something tells me this conversation might warrant one. "Mom, why did you never date anyone after Dad died? Was it because of me? Because you were a single parent?"

"What? No. That's ridiculous."

"Serena's scared I'll have to choose between her and Violet and she'll lose us both."

"Ah. I see." My hands tunnel in my hair. How does she get it so quickly when I still don't? "Care to share your thoughts? Because I'm stumped. I love her mom, so much, and she loves me. And Vi. God, we could be happy again, together, a fucking family. But she's scared and I'm scared, and I don't even know why!" My voice has risen in volume as I start to pace my kitchen and I stop, hoping I didn't wake my daughter. "I don't know what to do, Mom. How do I make her see I can love both her and Violet?"

"My sweet boy, you can't."

I sink down to the floor right where I am, letting my head fall into my empty hand.

"Until you realize you are more than a father, and you deserve to love and to be loved as a man, how can you expect Serena to realize the same?"

"What?" I ask, my voice broken with emotion. "I didn't say —"

"You didn't need to," Mom interrupts. "I know you. And I may have had a phone call from someone who loves you just as much as I do."

Aunt Claire. Of course, they've been talking.

"You're a generous, selfless, loyal, hardworking man, Leo Talbot, just like your father. But that's only a good thing until you take it too far and forget that you exist as an individual, not just as a police officer or as a father. If Serena is afraid of you choosing Violet over her, that just tells me she understands your job as Vi's dad is your most important job. And that makes me love that woman even more than I already did. But now you need to help her see that you love her and need her in your life just as much as you need Violet. And you do that by realizing you are enough for Violet exactly as you are. And letting yourself find happiness with Serena doesn't diminish that. If anything, it makes it grow because when you're happy and whole, you're the best version of yourself and the best father I know you can be."

Chapter Nineteen

Telling my friends and Leo about the studio took a weight off my shoulders in a way I didn't expect. No one had any magical solutions that can make all my worries disappear, but somehow, just knowing they're here for me is enough to give me some comfort and hope that I'll figure things out.

But that relief came at a cost. Because confessing everything to Leo while we were at the hot spring pool meant telling him about more than just my financial struggles. It meant admitting my fears of losing him again. Opening my heart up to love, especially with him, is scary shit. But the alternative? Not having him and Violet in my life? Even more terrifying.

Keeping me up all night, overthinking every decision I've made in the last twenty years terrifying.

Obsessing about the feel of his arms and how much I miss his warmth terrifying.

Picturing my life without him now that I've got another chance to be with him terrifying.

Finding a way through my fear is proving difficult, which is why I'm instead choosing to distract myself and keep busy.

"Why isn't your big, strong man helping us with this?" I drop another box of books down on the counter inside Paige's store. She looks up from the floor where she's been sorting her new inventory to restock shelves.

"You volunteered to assist me, so I informed Wyatt he could spend the day at Oceanside. I believe he's setting up storage racks for the kayaks that arrive this weekend."

"It was a rhetorical question, Paige." I wander over and sit down beside her. "Things are still good with you guys?"

My best friend's brow furrows. "Of course they are. I would have spoken to you had I any questions or concerns that I felt you could assist me with." She places a few more books on the shelf before looking at me again. "Wait. Is this one of those moments when your question was actually a reflection on something you wish to discuss about your own romantic situation?"

I let my head fall back against the shelf behind me with a thunk. "Maybe? I dunno."

Paige shifts around until she's parallel to me, leaning back against the shelves, our shoulders touching. "Are you still having some doubts about your relationship with Leo?"

"My life experiences may have left me jaded about love, but that's kept my heart safe for twenty years. But now Leo and Violet are making me wonder if a safe heart is worth the loneliness. I don't doubt his feelings for me. He says he loves me and I believe him. But I'm definitely having trouble believing it will last. Isn't that normal?"

"No. Not in my experience, it isn't."

"No?" I twist my head to face her. "You're telling me you never worry about things ending with Wyatt?"

To give her credit, Paige seems to consider my question seriously. Then again, she does everything seriously.

"I would be remiss if I ignored the fact that, yes, there was a time or two when I questioned if Wyatt truly loved me, but all I had to do was look at his actions and the way he treated me to know beyond a shadow of a doubt that what we have is real, authentic love. Now, whether that love will last forever? No one can ever truly know that. We are not omniscient, Serena. We are human beings. And human beings make mistakes, incorrect choices, and poor decisions. Life, or fate, whichever you choose to believe in, also plays a role. All you can do is have faith that what is meant to be will be. Enjoy the moment, as they say."

"I would have never said you'd be someone to put blind faith in anything."

"It's not blind. Not at all." Paige turns around and pulls a book off the shelf behind us, dropping it in my lap. It's a romance novel, but one I haven't read yet. "Why do you think we enjoy these books so much?"

"The really hot sex scenes?" I quip, but she just rolls her eyes at me.

"Romance novels put into words our deepest hopes and fantasies. Partners who accept us as we are, flaws and all. Passion, connection, commitment. A love that transcends space and time. These books let us pretend these things are guaranteed to everyone, even though our rational brains know that isn't always the case. But do you know why I personally enjoy them?"

I shake my head slowly.

"Because they teach forgiveness. Every couple goes through a dark moment, that instance or situation when they question everything, when all seems lost. But somehow, they find their way to the other side and learn to forgive not only their partner, but themselves. That's what love is to me. That up and down, but always finding your way back together. If it weren't for romance novels, I don't believe I would have been able to see the opportunity for true love when I was finally presented with it."

She taps the cover of the book, and I look down at it.

"You might want to read this one. It's about a divorced couple who reunite after several years and how they manage to rekindle their love, but more importantly, their trust." Paige stands up, dusting her hands on her pants. "I'm going to go next door for lunch. Can I bring you something as a thank you for helping me with the inventory?"

"No thanks," I mumble, distracted by Paige's wise words and the book in my hands.

"Alright. Then take that book as thanks. And Serena." I finally glance up from the cover. "If Leo is your opportunity for true love, don't let your decisions be fueled by fear. You deserve more than that."

That book sits on my desk all afternoon while I teach, my eyes going to it at every opportunity. I can't get what Paige said out of my head.

Don't let your decisions be fueled by fear.

God, is that how I've lived my life? Letting fear be in the driver's seat? For someone who prides herself on being strong and independent, that's an unsettling realization. But Paige is rarely, if ever, wrong.

When I finally get the studio locked up and make my way to my apartment, all I want to do is read. I'm not foolish enough to think a book holds all the answers, but Paige is pretty freaking smart. So if she says I should read it, then I want to read it.

I draw a hot bath, light some candles, and sink down into my tub to start reading.

And I don't stop until the water is cold and my skin is turning prune-y. Because goddamnit, Paige was right. It's as if I'm reading my own life story, in a way. And I'm desperate to see how it works out.

The other thing my genius friend was right about is the way romance novels teach forgiveness. Not being a doormat, but a true, authentic understanding of when you are standing in your own way.

Just like I am right now with Leo.

I towel off quickly, throw on my pajamas, and walk out to my kitchen, barely taking my eyes off the pages in front of me. The main couple, Georgia and Holden, have just had a conversation that echoes so much of what Leo and I talked about at the hot springs. The difference is, Georgia isn't walking away like I did. She's there, listening to him. Communicating like a freaking grownup. Working through their differences.

God, I'm such an idiot.

The vibration from my phone on the counter is an irritation I want to ignore, so I do. Until it starts up a second time, and I grab it without looking, annoyed and fully prepared to tell whoever it is to stop calling.

"Serena?"

That voice.

The book falls from my hands to the floor, forgotten the instant I hear his voice.

Even knowing this moment would come, courtesy of my mother's call, didn't really prepare me for it.

"Dad?" I choke out, somehow making my way over to my couch and sinking down.

"Hi, princess."

Oh God. I'm not ready for this. I don't know if I ever will be. "What...what do you want?"

I can hear him take a deep breath in. "Did your mother tell you I'd be calling?"

"Yes." I purposefully don't say anymore. I need to hear it from him, why he left, why he disappeared.

"Okay. Right. Wow, you'd think I'd be more ready for this." A pained chuckle comes down the line. "I've been thinking of calling you, planning it for months. Heck, years. And now I've got you on the phone and my mind is blank."

I stay silent, not giving him an inch.

"I guess I'll start with an apology. I owe you several, really. I had to leave back when I did, honey, trust me. It was for the best. But I never meant to stay away as long as I did."

"Then why did you?" I blurt out, unable to hold back.

"Oh, princess. I...I was having problems. Personal ones. I want to tell you everything, Serena, but this is hard for me. To admit that I failed you and your mom so badly." Another loud sigh. I bite my lip, letting the pain from that overshadow a scrap of the pain in my heart. "Can I see you? I need to explain everything in person. Please, honey. I'll come to you, wherever you want. Your mom said you're on Vancouver Island now, and I can be there in a couple of days. Just say you'll see me, please."

"I don't know if I can see you," I whisper. "You left me. Your daughter. You walked away and you didn't look back. What could you possibly say that would allow me to be okay with that?" Tears are streaming down my face openly now. My free hand twists the front of my sweater into a knot, squeezing it, needing something to hold on to.

"I had to do what your mother and I both thought was best for you. That's the only reason I left, princess. I swear to you. I know I should have reached out sooner, but I was so scared."

"Scared of what?"

"Of failing you again. Look, I know this all sounds so cryptic, and you have no reason to forgive me, but just hear me out. Can you do that one thing for me? Please."

Something about his broken voice weakens my resolve. That and my mom's words when she first mentioned he might call — *I think you need this.*

"Fine. I'll meet with you."

When I hang up after confirming his plan to come to town early next week, I feel raw inside. Like someone has taken my heart and scraped away the scars from my past, leaving exposed the damaged pieces. I know eventually they'll heal and this call was the first step.

But can I really handle what comes next?

Not alone.

Something this big needs more than a late night dance session to work through it all.

No matter how conflicted I am about where things are between us right now, I know I need him. So, with shaking hands, I press the button that will connect me to the one source of love and strength I desperately need right now.

"Leo? I need you."

Chapter Twenty

Leo

"What's wrong?"

I bolt off the couch, ready for anything. In all the time I've known her, I've never heard Serena sound like this — so broken.

"My dad just called."

"Shit. Do you need me? I can come over. Wait. Fuck." I hit my forehead with a groan. *Violet.* "Damn it, I'm sorry, Tippy. Vi's sleeping and it's too late for me to call my aunt. Maybe I could —"

"No, Leo," she lets out a painful laugh. "You can't leave your daughter just because I'm sad from a phone call."

It kills me hearing her minimize her feelings like that, just like it kills me that this is basically just proving her point from the other day at the hot springs.

I'm faced with the impossible choice: my daughter or my love. I have never resented Violet, but in this moment, I wish things were different. I wish there was some way I could be there for Serena while she's hurting.

"Okay, baby. I can't come over, but can we switch to video so I can see you? Let me be here for you somehow."

"Okay." She sniffs back a tear, then the line goes quiet. I sit back down, quickly switch over to video, and call her back. Sure enough, when her beautiful face fills the screen, her cheeks are red and her eyes are shining with tears.

"Hey, talk to me. What did your dad want?

"He wants to come to town and meet up with me."

"Now? When did you last see him?" Frowning, I try to remember the last time I saw Serena's dad. It was before we broke up, obviously, so my memory isn't clear. But from what she's told me, after her parents' divorce, it sounds like he made himself scarce.

"He came to graduation, but that's it. He was gone right after and I haven't seen him in person since." Serena casts her eyes downward, but the hurt in her voice is obvious.

Damn. My heart breaks for my girl. Close to twenty years without seeing her own father. I can't imagine going more than a couple of days without seeing Violet.

"So why now, after all this time? What could he possibly have to say to you?"

Serena's watery eyes meet mine through the phone screen as she lifts her shoulders in a shrug. "I don't know. My mom told me the other day that Dad left because he had a gambling problem or something. Not sure why he stayed away this whole time, so maybe that's what he wants to tell me."

"Holy shit. Seriously?"

She nods. "Yeah, apparently he almost blew through my dance school money."

My head tips back against the couch. "Damn." I lean forward again and look at her carefully. The tears have stopped, but she still looks, I don't know, lost somehow. "I wish I was there to hold you."

"Me too," she says softly.

I exhale slowly. Being torn in two directions like this really fucking sucks. "Want me to stay on the phone until you fall asleep?"

A small smile crosses her lips. "Like we used to do in high school?"

"Yeah," I chuckle. "Except this time we've got video calls."

Her head dips down slightly, then she looks back at me. "I'd like that."

I stand up and stretch my free arm, letting a yawn break free. "Okay. I'm gonna get ready for bed, then I'll call you back. Deal?"

"Deal."

I don't think I've ever gotten ready for bed so quickly before, not even when Violet was a baby. But when I call Serena back, she's already in bed, her head on a pillow that I wish mine was on as well.

"Next best thing to being with you, baby."

"Thank you, Leo." Her smile is a welcome sight.

"I'm always gonna be here for you, you know that. Even if it's not in person, I'm here. I've got you. You're not alone, Tippy. Not anymore."

When I see a tear spill from her eye, I frown. "Shit, babe, I'm sorry. I didn't mean to upset you."

"No, no, that's a happy tear." She wipes it away with a sniff. "I love you, Leo."

"And I love you. I'm glad you called me tonight."

"Me too."

Even after Serena's eyes drift closed and the phone falls to her mattress, I stay on the call, watching her sleep from afar.

I've had my life turned upside down exactly four times so far. The first was when my dad died. The second time when Serena broke up with me in high school. Then when Alexa told me she was pregnant, and then again when Alexa walked out on me and Violet.

Four moments in time that changed the course of my future dramatically. Four moments that could have led me in the opposite direction from where I am now. Yet despite all of that, all those moments that could have broken me, I can see now with perfect clarity that every turning point led me here. Led me back to Serena.

"Hey Vi, should we drop off some of those cookies you made yesterday for Serena?" I ask as I brush my daughter's hair up into two pigtails, just like she asked.

"Uh-huh," she mumbles around a bite of a granola bar I gave her to stop whining while I got her ready. She nods vigorously, making it pretty hard to work on her hair, but I've had plenty of practice over the years with a squirmy kid.

"Okay. Then let's get going so we can do that before I take you to Aunt Claire's house." I lift her down from the bathroom counter and take her hand to lead her into the kitchen where she helps me choose three cookies for Serena and puts them in a bag.

It still takes us forever to get out the door because Vi is at that age where she insists on doing everything herself, even the things she really can't, like putting her shoes on the right feet. But today, I don't care. Despite the emotional weight of last night, I feel great. I feel clear, connected, and ready to prove to Serena that she belongs with me and Vi.

I'll still give her whatever space and time she needs, but I'm also not going to let her doubt for one second that I'm in this for the long haul. She's mine. Ours.

We pull up outside the studio, and I've only got a few minutes to spare before I'm meeting my aunt at the police station so she can take Violet for the day. Thankfully, Serena must have either seen us coming or be on her way somewhere because she's locking the door of the studio when Violet calls out to her.

"Rena! Coo-tees!"

She turns around, startled, but I'm relieved to see she seems happier today, or at least tranquil.

"Hi, Miss Violet, what do you have there?" Serena drops down into a crouch as Violet barrels into her, the baggie of cookies smacking Serena lightly as Vi's arms wrap as far around her as they can. She stands up with my daughter in her arms, and finally, she looks at me.

"Hey Tippy," I say, giving her a slow, easy smile. Leaning in, I kiss her cheek, then take the bag from Violet's hands. "Vi wanted to bring you some cookies."

"Wow, thank you so much, Vi." Serena hugs my little girl in tight, and it's a struggle not to pull them both into my arms and never let go.

"Eat a coo-tee now?" Violet asks, and Serena and I both laugh.

"It's a little early for cookies, baby girl, and we have to get going to meet Aunt Claire."

Serena sets Violet down on the ground. "I'll see you soon at dance class, okay?"

She straightens and looks at me, her hand reaching out, then dropping back to her side as if she isn't sure what to do or how to act. I don't blame her, I don't know how affectionate to be in front of Violet. I've never had to consider that before, or wonder what she might think about me kissing a woman.

But damn, do I ever want to kiss Serena right now.

Before I can overthink it, I do just that. I press my lips to hers, briefly, but it's enough.

"I'll talk to you later, okay?" I say, pitching my voice low enough so that hopefully Violet doesn't hear. "It's good to see you smiling again."

Her arms wrap around me, squeezing briefly. "You two make it easy to smile, even with all the crazy in my life right now."

"Vi, we better go and meet Aunt Claire. C'mon kiddo." With one last heated glance in Serena's direction, I head off toward the police station with Violet skipping along beside me. "That made Serena happy, didn't it?"

"Yup. Daddy, I love Rena."

My feet stumble at those words. All this time I've been re-discovering my love for Serena, and somehow it never crossed my mind that my daughter could be falling for her as well. I'd be lying if I didn't admit I'm both happy and scared about that thought.

Happy because, obviously, the more people my daughter has around her that love her, care for her, and she cares for in return, the better. Having a female role model as strong and confident as Serena is nothing short of amazing.

But. And it's a pretty big *but.*

Violet's heart being involved means if things *don't* work out for any reason, I'm not the only one who will be devastated.

That's a risk I have to consider carefully.

"I'm telling you, man, the Monte Cristo sandwich is the bomb."

"I'll take your word for it."

Hunter Callaghan is like a golden retriever puppy. Nothing but youthful energy and overly friendly excitement. But he's also a damn good cop and a decent guy from what I know so far. He's new to Dogwood Cove, just like me, but fits in well at the station.

When he mentioned earlier that he was going to grab lunch at Camille's café, I decided to come along to grab a sandwich.

I had originally planned to take lunch back to my desk and keep reviewing procedural files, but that was before we walked in the door of the café.

"Hey cuz, what can I... Oh." Kat's mouth opens and closes. "H-hi Hunter."

"Hey, Kitty Kat. Got a table for two? I'm tryin' to convince Leo to join me for lunch. He doesn't believe the Monte Cristo is the best damn sandwich out there."

Kitty Kat? Jesus Christ, that's corny as fuck. Do her brothers know about this? I arch my brow at my cousin as we walk past, and she blushes furiously. Hunter might appear oblivious to her reaction to him, but I'm not blind.

Kat's got a crush.

"Look, man, I said I'd stay and eat here, but you're not getting me to eat a sandwich that has egg on it."

"Dude, it's like French toast and a grilled cheese sandwich had a baby. It's delicious."

Kat giggles — *giggles* — at that insane description.

"Sounds gross. Sorry. Kat, can I just get a chicken ranch wrap please?"

"Sure." She smiles at me before turning to Hunter and tucking her hair behind her ear. "And a Monte Cristo?"

"You know it." Hunter winks at her, then refocuses his attention on me. "So. How ya liking Dogwood Cove? I only moved here a few months before you, but I gotta say I like it so far. It's quiet, not a lot of action on the job, but it's cool. Is it boring for you though? Coming from Vancouver? This is my first job, as a cop I mean. It's a good place to start I think. But I guess I'll move to a bigger city someday. Maybe."

I sit there, sipping my water, smiling and nodding as Hunter rambles on. But my mind is down the street with a certain blonde dance teacher.

Not with the fucking golden retriever I'm having lunch with.

"Oh, did you hear about what's going on over in Westport?" Hunter asks, taking a drink from his water.

I shake my head, still distracted by thoughts of Serena.

"It's crazy. They're a bigger city than us, but still, never expected something like this. Last week, someone went around at nighttime throwing bricks through the windows of random businesses. The weird part is they aren't taking anything or doing anything else."

That gets my attention. "Seriously? Any leads on who or why?"

"Nope. It seems completely random so far. I have a buddy on the force over there and he said they're totally confused.

Something like seven businesses were hit in two nights, and then nothing since. They're starting to wonder if it was just some local kids causing trouble or a prank gone overboard."

"Seems a bit extreme for troublemakers. I'll talk with the chief about stepping up night patrols."

Hunter groans good-naturedly. "I had a feeling you might say that. Bring on the overtime night shifts."

I push away from the table and stand, dropping some money to cover lunch. "Hey, you're the one who told the deputy chief about a potential threat. You brought this on yourself, my man."

I slap him on the shoulder, wave at Kat, and head out into the sunny afternoon, my footsteps carrying me down the sidewalk to the dance studio automatically.

Standing outside, I watch her for a few minutes. She's got a group of little kids in there, but it's not Violet's class. Still, her beauty and passion for dance is evident, even from a distance. Eventually, duty calls, and I make my way back to the station.

But not without wondering how, or when, I can get Serena to myself again. My body and soul crave her, and my heart is desperate for another chance to show her I'm in this forever.

Chapter Twenty-One

Serena

The chatter of women fills the studio, different from the normal noise and chaos of my younger students. I'm trying to seem busy, fiddling with the sound system, but the reality is, I'm nervous.

It's the first adult intro to ballet class tonight. And while I might have brushed it off with my friends as just being frustrating having to teach adults, the truth is, it raises a lot of self-doubt and insecurity in me. Kids don't judge the same way adults do. They don't know when you mess up or fail.

It's harder to hide mistakes from grown-ups.

My friends all wanted to sign up, and honestly, I would have loved to have them here, taking some of the pressure off. But to my surprise, the interest in this class was so high I had to start a wait list. Which meant my friends had to pass for now since pulling in new students is the priority.

Turning around, I survey the room. There are a few familiar faces from town, some mothers of current students, but there's a lot of people I don't know. Apparently Ashley's idea to advertise in Westport was a good one.

Closing my eyes, I take one last second to center myself, and to my surprise, Violet's face pops into my head. Thinking of her and how shy she was at first is exactly what I need to find my own inner courage the same way she did.

"Alright everyone, let's form three rows facing the mirror, and we'll begin with a simple warm up."

I'm a little taken aback when they all immediately quiet down and listen to my instruction. "Great, thanks. Umm, well, I'm Serena. I guess you guys know that." I laugh awkwardly, but the women in front of me just smile.

Find your freaking backbone, Serena.

"So, we'll be together for the next eight weeks, learning the basics of ballet, jazz, and a little hip-hop. I should be upfront with you all that my specialty is ballet, so please don't expect great things when we get to hip-hop."

There's a light laugh, and it helps me relax. I got this. Maybe grown-ups aren't so terrifying to teach.

"By the end of the set of classes, my plan is for you to have learned some basic choreography that we'll put together in sort of a freestyle dance. Just for fun, no recital or anything. But yeah. Hopefully, it'll be a good time."

I get a smattering of applause, and plenty of smiles, and finally, I'm feeling excited to teach. I turn to the sound system and press play on my usual warm-up playlist.

"Let's begin with some stretches and basic movements. Put your heels together, toes turned out, in first position."

Just like that, my mind and body go into dance mode. Turns out, teaching adults isn't all that different from children. I give many of the same corrections and encouragements and lead them through a very similar set of exercises and movements. When I finally glance at the clock, I'm shocked to see our hour is up.

"Wow, ladies, well done for our first night together."

"Are we ballerinas now?" a woman calls out from the back row. I bite back what would be my usual sarcastic response in favour of a tilt of my head with a small smile, letting the other women's laughter do the work for me.

"Next week we'll work on some more basic positions and movements, and then try putting them together."

"Thanks, Serena, this was a lot of fun," one of the ladies from town, Mary, I think her name is, says as she walks out of the studio.

"Yeah, who knew at my age I could learn something new?"

"I'm so glad you're finally offering classes for us."

"Your ad popped up at the perfect time; I was looking for something new to try."

I smile, nod, and wave as everyone offers their thanks and praise as they get ready to go. I'm thrilled the response is so overwhelmingly supportive and positive. But once they're all gone and I turn the lock on the studio door, I sag against it.

It's late, later than I normally finish teaching, and I'm exhausted. Physically and mentally.

I go onto autopilot with my closing up tasks, my brain foggy with fatigue. My sole focus is getting this done and falling into bed.

At first, when the sound of smashing glass startles me from my almost-asleep state, I think it must be a dream. Then the alarm goes off and I bolt upright in bed.

Fumbling for my phone, I manage to dial 911 as I race to the door to my apartment and double check the locks on it.

My heart is racing.

I feel like I can't take in a full breath.

When the operator comes on the line, I barely manage to blurt out that I think someone has broken into my studio before the tears start falling and I start sobbing deep, ragged breaths.

I want Leo. I need him to make me feel safe. But the operator won't let me off the phone until I can hear the police sirens.

The sound of boots pounding up the stairs to my apartment sends a fresh wave of panic through my body until I hear the voice that accompanies the banging on my door.

"Serena! Tippy! Let me in, baby, it's me."

I fly over to the door, dropping my phone onto the floor. As soon as it's open just a crack, Leo flings it open and grabs me.

"You're okay. You're okay. I'm here, baby, you're safe." I can barely hear his murmured words of comfort over my own deep sobs.

But the tight band of his arms around my body is slowly easing the panic in my chest. The buzzing noise in my head, adrenaline induced panic I guess, starts to subside and I become aware of other things. The sound of voices downstairs, the flash of lights outside, the crackle of Leo's radio, and the damp feeling on my neck where his face is pressed into my skin.

That proves to be enough to settle my fears so I can draw back slightly to look at him. His eyes are red rimmed, and the mixture of terror and relief on his face mirrors my own.

"Leo."

That's all I manage before I crumple again. Leo sweeps me up into his arms and carries me to the couch before sitting down with me in his lap. His belt is poking into me, but I don't care.

He's here. I'm safe.

The inevitable crash that follows an adrenaline spike like I just had hits me hard. I want to burrow into Leo's chest and ignore whatever just happened. But that's wishful thinking.

"Tippy, we need to go downstairs."

"What happened?" I croak out.

"A brick was thrown through the front window."

That sends me jolting into standing. "What? Oh my God. Why?!"

Leo comes up beside me and takes my hand in his. "Not sure. As soon as we pulled up and I saw it, I ran to find you. I'm so fucking glad you're okay and you weren't down there." He pulls me back into his arms, and I realize he's still shaking.

"Leo, I'm fine. I was asleep."

"I know. I just...just... Give me a minute, okay? This is hitting a little close to home, that's all." His voice cracks, and it dawns on me this must be stirring up some horrible memories for Leo, given what happened to his dad.

And just like that, my terror spikes again at all of the what-ifs.

What if I had been downstairs doing one of my late-night dances that I do when I can't sleep or need to think things through? What if my apartment door had been unlocked? What if the sound hadn't woken me up or the alarm hadn't gone off or whoever it was had tried to come upstairs?

Suddenly, I don't feel so fine anymore.

We stay locked together for several moments, both of us needing the security of holding on to each other.

But I know I have to see for myself what's happened. Somehow, I manage to disentangle myself from Leo and step away, heading toward the door leading down to the studio.

"Wait. Baby." Leo tugs me back, and I turn to look at him. "You need shoes." He points down at my bare feet. "And maybe some clothes so I don't have to murder my coworkers for seeing you like that."

A laugh bursts free from me, and I think we're both grateful for the break in the tension from tonight's unexpected excitement.

"I'll just go and get dressed, then." I move to walk to my bedroom, but Leo won't let go of my hand. When I glance at him questioningly, his lips quirk up in a wry grin.

"Maybe I should stand watch. In the interest of personal safety, of course."

I let out a shaky laugh. Because now that the initial panic has worn off, I can appreciate that Leo is in full uniform, in my apartment, for the first time since the night he had to take off because Violet was sick.

"Let's save this moment for when your coworkers aren't all downstairs dealing with my vandalized dance studio."

"Good call." He shoves his hands in his pockets and leans against the door frame of my bedroom. "But I'll still keep watch. Just in case."

I roll my eyes and make quick work of getting dressed, grabbing the first things I find and pulling them on over the giant T-shirt I sleep in. It's only when I hear a strangled noise come from the doorway that I realize two things.

One, I forgot underwear, so Leo just got a full-on ass shot, and two, the hoodie I grabbed happens to be his from high school.

"I always wondered where that sweatshirt went," he says in a low voice.

I keep my back to him, unable to look him in the eyes just now. "You're not getting it back."

"I don't want it back. I want *you* back. You happen to come with my favourite hoodie, which is purely a bonus."

His hands land on my shoulders, and he slowly turns me around.

"Besides, you always did look better in it than me."

Lifting up on my toes, I kiss the corner of his mouth lightly, but Leo has other plans. With a growl, he wraps his hands in my hair and drags my lips to his for a crushing kiss.

"Hey boss — oh, sorry. Sorry. Didn't mean to interrupt. Umm... "

We break apart and Leo spins around with a scowl on his face. "Callaghan, what do you need?" he barks out at the younger officer, wrapping his arm around my shoulders.

"We just need Miss Matheson, umm, Serena, to come downstairs and give her statement."

"Have we found any clues that might help us figure out who did this?"

The poor man's face turns bright red, and I squeeze Leo's side to try and get him to dial down the intensity.

"No, sir. No prints yet, and no tire tracks, either. We don't have traffic cams to review, but I'm guessing whoever it was must have come on foot and left immediately after. Maybe they parked on a side street. We can canvas the houses on nearby streets to see if anyone noticed anything, but it looks a lot like those cases over in Westport, to be honest."

"We don't know that, Officer, so let's not jump to conclusions. This could have gone a lot worse if Serena had been downstairs. I want guys patrolling the neighborhood all night."

"Leo, calm down," I murmur. "I'm fine, and it's just a window."

"Well, actually, you might want to come and take a look." Callaghan scratches his head ruefully. "Just make sure you have shoes on."

Leo arches his brow at me at that last comment and I just roll my eyes in return. Shoes on, we make our way downstairs.

When I finally see the destruction to my studio, I can't hold back my tears of dismay. The brick went straight through the large picture window that looks right into the dance space. Shattered glass is everywhere, and the beautiful wood floor is destroyed where the brick landed.

"Thank fuck you weren't down here doing one of your late-night dance sessions." Leo speaks so quietly I almost don't hear him.

I jolt at his comment. "I forgot you knew about that."

A half-hearted chuckle comes out. "Are you kidding? I remember sneaking onto the football field with you the night before exams so you could dance away your nerves. You've always used movement to work through anything heavy. And if you'd been down here tonight doing that... " Leo shudders as his voice trails off.

I wrap my arms around my stomach as reality sinks in. He might be thinking about the risk to me, but I'm thinking about the risk to my business. I won't be able to teach in the space until, at the very least, the glass is cleaned up. Even then, how long does it take for a window to be replaced? That's a big fucking window. Oh man, and the floor. I can just see the girls landing wrong and hitting that divot in the floor. Shit, I need the floor repaired before I can have a class. Oh God. This is going to take weeks.

"Babe. Babe?" Leo's voice breaks through my internal freak-out and I spin to him.

"Leo, what am I going to do? I can't afford to shut down for weeks while waiting for repairs. Oh my God, my insurance is going to take forever to come through, I don't have the money for any of this, and I'm going to have to cancel so many classes. Shit. My mortgage payments! Oh fuck."

"Serena, stop!"

At his almost shout, everyone in the studio freezes.

"Guys, give us the room for a few minutes." Leo looks sharply at the other two officers in turn, and they immediately leave.

"Well, that was embarrassing," I snap, still vibrating with overwhelm.

"I don't give a fuck," he barks back. His hands cover his face, then slide down to his hips. "Why are you freaking out about repairs and insurance right now? Do you not understand how serious this could have been? You could have been down here and been hit by the fucking brick. Goddamnit, Tippy, money doesn't matter. *You* do."

I open my mouth to respond, but Leo starts pacing in front of me, continuing his tirade.

"I can't lose you again, Serena. Fucking hell, Violet can't lose you. She's lost so much already. And she loves you. We love you.

Fuck, if something had happened to you." His voice breaks and it takes all the wind out of my sails.

I wrap my arms around him from behind and press my cheek to his back. I can feel the thump, thump, thump of his heart, and I know it's beating for me.

"I need you, Tippy. We both need you. You can't... This... God."

He pivots in my arms, drops to his knees, and crushes his arms around my waist, like he needs to feel me against him, to know I'm okay and I'm here with him. My hand immediately starts stroking his hair, and I'm murmuring words; I don't even know what they are.

Leo loves me.

Violet loves me.

He's right, money doesn't matter nearly as much as love, family, and happiness. And I have all three of those things right in front of me.

The last piece of defensive wall that surrounded my heart crumbles to dust. Leo's vulnerability, his honesty, his genuine love and commitment to me, it's never been more clear to me than it is in this moment.

I sink down to my knees, fitting myself in between his.

"I'm sorry, Leo."

He looks up, and when I see the tears tracking down his cheek, my thumb lifts to wipe them away.

"I'm sorry I scared you or made you think I didn't appreciate the severity of what happened tonight. I do. I just got caught up in worrying about the other stuff because my brain can't process the rest of it. They smashed a window in my studio, but they could have come up to my apartment next, and that's terrifying. I just... I can't go there yet."

Leo rests his forehead on mine. "I'm sorry, too. I freaked out on you when what you need is for me to stay calm. But the thought of anything happening to you is so fucking scary. I can't live without you. I *won't* live without you."

"You don't have to."

I'm crying now and I know we need to get up off the floor and finish dealing with everything, and I know Leo has to go back to work, but all I want to do is stay in his arms forever.

Which is why, when he turns on his radio to speak with his coworkers, I'm flooded with relief and love for this man who knows me better than I know myself.

"Callaghan, Moritz, I'm taking Serena back to my house for the night. I'll send someone over to help put boards up; you can stay on site until they get here. And then I'm taking off the rest of my shift."

He doesn't wait for their reply, just pulls out his phone and thumbs out a text. Within minutes, there's a reply, but when I go to look at who he's messaging, he doesn't let me see.

"Baby, all I want you to do is go upstairs and pack a bag with a few days' worth of clothes and whatever else you need. You're staying with me and Vi."

"But... "

"No buts." He cups my face in his hands and kisses me. "I need to hold you tonight, okay?"

Chapter Twenty-Two

Leo

Adrenaline is still coursing through my veins as Serena and I walk over to my patrol car. The text I sent to my cousins has them en route to put up plywood over the window, and another message sent to the chief has given me clearance to leave. Thank fuck for small towns.

"I can't believe you just walked out on your shift."

I lean into the car where I've just settled Serena in the passenger seat and lift her hand to my mouth so I can press my lips to it. "What is it going to take for you to believe that I would do anything for you?" I ask quietly. Then, closing the door, I give a quick nod to my coworkers before jogging around to the driver's side.

"But what about Violet?"

I take Serena's face in my hands and stare straight into her eyes. "I already texted Aunt Claire and asked her to keep Vi away from the house tomorrow morning. You need me, and I need to be here for you. So *let me* be here for you."

Her eyes brim with tears, but they don't spill over. Instead, she gives me a shaky nod, and I make myself turn my attention to the road to get us the fuck home.

The drive back to my house is silent. I'm white-knuckling the steering wheel as I try to sort out the mess in my head. When my partner and I pulled up to the studio and I saw the smashed window, my heart stopped. It was like I was reliving the memories of losing my dad all over again. Only this time, it wasn't just a story I was being told by his partner. It was real time, real life, and it was the woman I love more than just about anything who could have been hurt — or worse.

When I pull into my driveway and kill the engine, I turn to Serena, only to see her tucked up against the door, her eyes closed.

"Tippy, we're here."

She stirs, blinking at me with tired eyes, and I'm hit with a tsunami-sized wave of love. Making my way around the car I open the door to help Serena out of the car. Quickly grabbing her bags from the back seat, I take her hand, and we walk up to my front door. I don't let go of her as I juggle the bags to get my key in the lock and open the door.

Once we're inside, I lead her straight up the stairs and into my bedroom. It's the first time she's been in here, and some other time I'll take the opportunity to see her reaction, how she fits in my space. But right now, I need to care for my girl.

I help her undress, then pull back the blanket so she can climb into bed. Then, as quickly as I can, I lock up my firearm and duty belt and dump my uniform in a pile beside the bed before crawling in and pulling her into my arms.

"Sleep. You're safe."

The exhale of relief I hear from her as she snuggles in underneath my arms soothes a part of me that has been on edge ever since we pulled up to the studio.

She is mine, and I will protect her.

I have no clue what time it is when I feel Serena climb on top of me, but it's just barely light out, so it's early. Not too early for my dick to take notice of her sliding down my body and taking me in her mouth.

"Serena? Wha-What?" I say groggily as she sucks me in deep. "Oh, shit. Baby."

Her tongue laps up my length and swirls around the tip of me. I'm still not sure if I'm awake or just dreaming as I haul her up and flip us over so her hair spreads out over my pillow.

Fuck, that's a beautiful sight.

My hand grazes the side of her body before I grab her thigh and lift it around my waist. Our kiss is sloppy, both of us drowsy enough to not have complete control of our movements. But when I slide into her heat, she welcomes me, her body clenching around my cock almost instantly.

In the dim light of whatever ungodly hour it is, we come together, seeking that undeniable connection and comfort. I'll happily give this to her whenever she needs it.

"Leo," she whispers against my skin. "Where are your handcuffs?"

My entire body contracts at her words. "My handcuffs?" My brain is a mess, an overwhelming combination of tired, aroused, and now... curious.

She pushes against my chest, flipping our positions again so she's back on top. Her pelvis starts to move, grinding down onto my cock. It's distracting, but not as much as the words she says next.

"Yeah. I want you to use them on me."

I grip her ass to still her motion, locking my eyes on hers. "Tippy, are you sure? I thought after last time you didn't— "

She stops me with a finger to my lips.

"You chose me above anything else tonight. I want to show you that I will always choose you. Love you. *Trust you*."

"You don't have to let me handcuff you to show me that you trust me, baby."

Her hips start to move again and I let her, stifling my groan. "I know I don't *have* to, but what if I *want* to? I need this Leo; I need you. There's so much hard stuff going on right now, I need something easy. Something happy. Something loving. I need you."

I run my hands up the side of her body to her neck. "I do love you, Serena Matheson. And if it's within my power, I'll always give you whatever you want or need."

Serena carefully lifts off of me, stretching out on the bed beside me, her body curving and twisting on my sheets. I can't take my eyes off her.

"Leo." She arches her brow at me, and I realize I've been staring.

She slowly reaches her arms up above her head, grabbing on to my headboard. Her back arches with the movement and those luscious tits are pushed up.

"Cuff me, Officer."

I've never heard three words sound so fucking hot in my life. I scramble to get up and out of bed, going to my closet where the safe is located that holds my tactical gear. It takes two tries to get the code in right, but finally, I'm holding the cuffs in my hand. Setting the key down carefully on my bedside table, I climb back on the bed. My dick is rock-hard, painfully so, in anticipation of what's about to happen.

"Are you sure about this?" I ask gently. "Because I only want it if you do. I love you, and I know you love me, and that's more than enough for me right now."

Serena sits up, bringing her hands to the top of my legs. My dick twitches at the proximity, but she doesn't touch me.

"Leo Talbot. I trust you with my body, with my heart, and with my life. And I want you to tie me up and take control of my body. I want you to give me more pleasure than I've ever had in my life. I want this. I've thought about it ever since that first day I saw you in your uniform, and I'm done fantasizing about it, I want the real thing."

Slowly she lays back down, once again stretching her arms up and over her head. The pure beauty of this moment stuns me as I take in the sight. The love of my life laid out on my bed, her golden blonde hair spread on my pillow, and her heart fully open to me.

I slowly open the cuffs, watching her face carefully. Any hint she isn't into this and I'll stop. It doesn't matter that I'm harder than I've ever been before or that this feels like every fucking fantasy I've ever had come to life. Her love, trust, and comfort are more important than my deep primal desire.

The click of the cuffs closing around her delicate wrists pierces the silence, followed immediately by her audible inhale.

"They're cold," she murmurs as I run my hands up and down her arms.

"Metal," I say absently. "Are you okay?"

Serena nods, licking her lips. "I am. I could be better, though."

"Oh yeah?"

"Mm-hmm."

I position myself over her, letting my cock slide between her legs. "Is this what you're missing?"

"God, yes," she pants, eyes closed and hips lifting, seeking, searching me out.

I lower my head and kiss her softly. "Look at me, Tippy."

Her gorgeous hazel eyes flutter open, and the love and trust I see in them is staggering.

"Keep your hands up there, baby," I say gruffly, loving her enthusiastic nod.

Slowly I notch my dick at her entrance and slide in and out, keeping my thrusts shallow at first until Serena is squirming and panting underneath me.

"Oh my God, Leo, please just…just… "

"Just this?" I growl, slamming into her. Serena cries out my name, meeting every move of my hips with a lift of her own.

"Yes!"

She's good, keeping her hands above her head, and I love watching her fists clench and then release, mimicking the sensations lower down. I rock in and out of her, twisting my hips occasionally, never letting her get used to what I'm doing. Her moans start to increase in volume and intensity, and I can feel my orgasm thundering down my spine.

It's too soon. I need her to come at least once before I do. Maybe twice.

I pull out and ignore her groan of protest. When her hands start to come down, I lift them up and pin them above her head.

"Stay there, baby."

"Leo, please."

"Fuck, I love hearing you beg. Don't worry, baby, I've got you."

Sliding down her body, I relinquish her wrists only to lift her legs over my shoulders and dive into her luscious sex with my tongue, lapping up all of the moisture leaking from her. I let my tongue mimic the motions of my dick, swirling around her clit, dipping in between her folds. But when I latch onto the tip of her clit and suck, her hands drop down, scratching at my back as she comes with an explosive cry.

Letting her legs drop down off my shoulders, I take her hands and thread our fingers together before slowly lifting them back up over her head. Holding them there with one hand, I drag the fingers of my other one down her face, over her breasts, teasing her stiff nipples before kissing her firmly. Her teeth latch onto my lower lip lightly, enough to make me groan.

My cock slams back into her as I shout her name. This time, our pace is frantic. Both of us desperate to reach the finish line in the biggest and best way possible.

"Hold on, Tippy," I growl when she wraps her legs around my waist. She squeezes them, and I feel the answering clench of her around my cock.

"Holy shit. Yes, baby. Let me feel you come all over me."

"Oh God, Leo!"

Serena starts to convulse around me, her body spasming through her release. My thrusts get even more intense, erratic, uncontrolled, and then suddenly I'm shouting her name, shooting into her with everything I have.

Eventually, I slow down, rocking into her lightly, until I finally come to a stop. My arms are shaky, but I hold myself up, not letting all of my weight crush Serena.

Then her arms drift down over my back and the feel of the cold metal startles me.

"Damn. I'm sorry, let me get those off of you."

But when I slowly untangle myself and get a look at her face, Serena doesn't look uncomfortable at all. She's got this dreamy, just fucked, perfectly content expression all over, and I'll be damned if it doesn't make me want to take her again.

Grabbing the key, I unlock the cuffs, swearing under my breath when I see how red her wrists are. I lift them to my lips and press soft kisses all over.

"I love you, baby. But maybe next time we use something a little softer."

Her gaze lands on me and turns ever so slightly wicked. "I dunno, I kind of liked the little bite of pain mixed with the pleasure."

Letting my body fall to the side of her, I groan. "That's dangerous for me to hear."

She cuddles into my side. "Thank you for everything tonight, Leo."

I lift my head to stare down at her. "What the fuck, Serena, don't thank me for doing my job, or for loving you. That's...that's just...no."

Serena pokes me, then presses a kiss to the spot she just jabbed. "Okay, geez, don't sound so offended."

I pull her in even tighter to my body. "Then don't say crazy stuff like that."

Eventually, her breathing evens out, and we fall asleep again just like that. With the early morning light filtering in and with our bodies and souls satisfied.

Something about seeing Serena barefoot in my kitchen, wearing nothing but my old high school hoodie, feels so goddamn good. It's sexy as fuck, but it's also more than that. It's a settled feeling in my soul and a steady sense of completeness running through my veins. This is all I've wanted, ever since I first met her so many years ago.

But something is not quite right. The room is way too silent.

I walk over to where Serena stands, facing my kitchen counter, stirring a cup of tea for a lot longer than necessary. I take the spoon out of her hands, set it on the counter, and turn her so she's facing me. Tucking her into my body, I rest my chin on the top of her head.

"What's wrong? And don't say nothing because I know that's a lie. You're quiet, and Serena Matheson is rarely quiet, unless something heavy is on her mind."

She laughs, but it sounds strained, and I frown.

"I'm fine, Leo, honestly. It's nothing to worry about right now."

I pull back slightly and cup her face in my hands. "How 'bout you let me decide if I'm going to worry about something. And right now, I'm worried about you. Are you still processing what happened last night? You know you can stay here as long as you need to. Hell, forever would be fine."

"We are *not* talking about me moving in yet, okay?"

Her kiss softens the blow of that statement, but only slightly. Because the truth is, I want her here every goddamn day for the rest of our lives.

"Fine. Then what is it?"

"Geez, okay, okay. Stop the interrogation, I'll talk."

Satisfied, I step back in and wrap my arms around her again. She doesn't speak right away, but I wait her out.

"There's just a lot right now, you know?"

I nod, knowing she can feel the motion.

"And as much as I want to admit I'm totally in over my head, barely keeping up with the game of emotional whack a mole going on inside of my mind, I'm also terrified to do that."

"Why?" I can't help but ask.

I feel her shrug. "Because ever since I moved here, I've been the *strong one*. The independent, don't need nobody, especially not a man, take charge kind of woman. That's not the type of person who openly admits they're drowning under the weight of too much responsibility."

"I disagree," I say softly. "That's *exactly* the kind of person who does that. Because admitting when you need help, when you need someone to lean on, *that* is true strength."

Serena tilts her head up to look at me, a knowing expression on her face. "You sound like that's a lesson you've recently learned yourself."

"Yeah, it is," I answer honestly. "It took coming here, letting my family help me with Violet, and letting *you* help me with Violet to help me realize that it doesn't make me any less of a father if I don't do it all myself."

Serena doesn't say anything for a minute or two, but there's no rush to fill the silence. So much has happened in the last twenty-four hours, I can tell she needs some time to sort through her thoughts.

"Being here with you, it feels so good, so right. This is almost everything I've ever wanted, and yet I feel guilty that I'm so happy, especially after last night." She nuzzles in closer, and I kiss the top of her head.

"You have nothing to feel guilty about, Tippy. But what do you mean by almost everything?"

I feel the rise and fall of her chest. "Having you in my life again, being free to love you again, it's a dream come true. Yet, I can't help but feel like I'm trading one dream for another because I'm terrified I'm going to lose my dance studio. I'm running out of time. And now the repairs that are needed after last night — I don't have the money or the time to wait for insurance to pay. But I also don't know if I could find a buyer without fixing things. And if I lose the studio, I lose dance."

I hold her a little bit tighter. "Not gonna lie, it feels damn good hearing you say being with me is a dream come true. But I get it, baby. I get why you feel guilty for being happy, even though I wish you didn't. Because you deserve to be happy. And I hope you know I'll do whatever I can to help you save the studio because that studio *is* you. Teaching might not have been your first choice, but honestly, you're incredible at it."

Her face tips up to mine, and our lips meet in a soft kiss. I finally feel some of the tension ease from her body.

"Thank you. Seriously, being with you, having your strength in my life, it does make it easier to bear all of this. The thing is, I love teaching as much as I loved dancing professionally. Truthfully, I did envision myself opening a studio eventually. I just figured I'd have longer as a professional ballerina first. But now all of that is on the line."

I hate that the conversation has shifted its focus onto something this depressing, but maybe she's right, and losing the studio is almost a foregone conclusion. If that's the case, all I can do is hope that she'll lean on me for emotional support or more. No matter what, I'll be here with her throughout whatever happens.

"Do you think the studio would sell quickly?"

"Yeah, I know it will. There's someone down in Victoria that came around last year asking if I wanted a partner. I said no at the time, but they emailed me again a couple of months ago asking if anything had changed. I'm guessing if I reached out, they would buy it up quick."

"Would they let you stay on as teacher?"

"Maybe." She shrugs, and I can tell the nonchalance she's trying to convey is faint, at best. "Even if they didn't let me teach, I'm not going anywhere. Dogwood Cove is home."

My head falls forward, heavy with relief. And now it's Serena's turn to cup my face, forcing me to look at her.

"You're my home, Leo. You and Violet. I believe you'll help me figure this out, and no matter what, I'm not going anywhere."

The lightness in my heart and my head makes me dizzy with an impulsive need to show her how I feel hearing that. My hands go down to her ass, and I lift Serena up, spin around, and set her on the table — thankfully, it's not covered in the usual mess of crayons, sippy cups, and paper.

"Leo, what are you doing?" She laughs, and that sound is music to my ears.

"Making it clear to you that I'm not going anywhere, either."

I drop to my knees, push her legs open firmly, and lean in to kiss her inner thigh.

Her sultry moan and her hands tangling in my hair send my lips higher. I bite down gently, right at the crease of her hip, then suck just enough so that I know it'll leave a mark. I *want* to mark her. Claim her. Make it clear she is mine forever.

"Oh God." She tugs on the strands of my hair unintentionally, but fuck, does that bite of pain feel good.

I lift my head slightly so I can meet her gaze, my hands gripping the tops of her thighs, my thumbs slowly sweeping closer and closer to where I know she wants me.

"I want you to take what you need, baby. I want you to know I'm here for you, that it's okay to need me, to want me, to *use* me. I'm yours, Serena."

Her eyes widen, then fill with a lusty haze. Goddamn, she's beautiful.

"Leo," she murmurs, and I know from the decadent tone of her voice that she's right where I want her to be. Her grip on my head tightens again, and I let her move my head down. Her long legs lift up and drape over my shoulders, and her heels dig in, pushing my body forward.

Going down on Serena when she's wearing nothing but my high school sweatshirt is undoubtedly the hottest thing I have ever done with her. Hell, with any woman.

Serena taking control of it all?

Even hotter.

My tongue sweeps out, and I'm engulfed in the taste and scent of her arousal. Her legs squeeze the sides of my head as she holds me firmly, right where she wants me.

It's exactly where I want to be as well.

I lap at her, licking her entire slit before focusing on her clit. It's my sole purpose in this moment to get her off with nothing but my tongue. To prove to her that I've got her, that my hands will always hold her up, my mouth will always worship her, and my heart will always love her.

And when I suck her clit in between my teeth, letting them graze lightly over her sensitized skin, the sound of her screaming my name is the best sound in the world.

It's a sound I want to hear again and again for the rest of my life.

CHAPTER TWENTY-THREE

Serena

"I'm nervous. This is stupid. Why the hell am I doing this?"

Mila, Summer, and Paige are all sitting on my couch, watching me pace the small distance in front of my coffee table. Their expressions range from amused to thoughtful to compassionate.

No surprise who's wearing each face.

"Serena, I recognize he is your father, but he is also just a man. Why can you not treat him as such? Pretend he is a stranger come to discuss a trivial matter. Separate your emotions from the reality of the situation."

"Paige," Summer says gently, her eyes on me. "I don't think this is the time for logic. Speaking from my own experience, if my dad and I had managed to reconnect before he died, I think I would be a nervous wreck, also."

"Thank you." I sink down to the floor, lying on my back with my legs crossed. It's a weird position, but I find it comfortable and grounding. "I don't know, guys, I just can't figure out why he wants to see me now. God. What if he has another family he wants me to meet?" I sit upright, suddenly nauseous. "What if he replaced me and my mom with someone else. What if he —"

"Oh my God, stop." Mila throws her hands up in the air. "Serena, we love you. Seriously. Majorly. Big time. But you are spiraling and out of all of us, you are *not* the one who spirals. So snap out of it, babe, put on your big girl panties and do this."

Unconventional as it is, Mila's pep talk seems to work. Because she's right about at least one thing.

"I'm not spiraling. I don't spiral." I sit up and turn to face my friends. "Okay, maybe I'm spiraling a little, but you're right, this isn't me."

"To be fair, you're also still dealing with all the drama from the other night."

"I adore you and your sensitive soul, Summer, but I'm fine. Honestly. Leo said they're working with the Westport Police to see if my break-in was connected to a series of vandalisms over there, but so far it seems like a one-off thing. At the end of the day, I'm safe."

"And the studio?" Summer murmurs, her face still etched in concern. I appreciate it, but it's also kind of annoying me right now. I don't want to dwell on the bad stuff in my life. I want to get today over with and move forward with Leo and our future.

"The studio will sell, and hopefully, I'll stay on to teach without the cloud of debt over my head."

"I wish Ethan and I could buy it and rent it to you, but we just don't have the investment capital."

I reach over and grab Mila's hand, squeezing it gratefully. "I know you do, but really, it's okay. This isn't what I wanted, but it'll be fine. I have you guys, and I have Leo and Violet. I don't need anything else."

"Do you want us to come with you to meet your dad?"

I rise to standing. "No, I can do this. Thanks for bringing breakfast, Mila. I'll let you guys know how everything goes."

One by one my friends stand, and after a round of hugs, they leave and I'm alone.

With a long, slow exhale, I let my eyes close. A memory of one of the last times I saw him comes to my mind.

I was seventeen, and it was after a dance recital. Leo came home with us for hot chocolate, which was our family tradition ever since I was small. Looking back, I've been able to reconcile the memory of Dad acting weird that night, not as affectionate or happy as normal, with the knowledge that he was slowly distancing himself.

The question is, which man am I meeting today — the loving father who learned how to do a perfect ballet bun or the father who disappeared to deal with his demons and never looked back?

My phone vibrates on the table in the living room.

Maybe he's cancelling. That makes me feel like a terrible person. Why can't I be, if not excited, at least curious about this?

LEO: You sure you want to meet him alone... I'll fake a migraine and get out of the rest of my shift if you need me to.

My heart fills as I type out my response.

SERENA: I'm fine, honestly. I need to do this alone. Don't know why, I just do. Besides, you already left work once for me, not sure it looks good for the new deputy chief to be shirking his responsibilities like that. But I love you for offering.

LEO: Nothing is more important to me than you right now. Certainly not my job. I'm here if you need me, no matter what. Hell even if you don't need me you just need a hug. I'm good at hugs, or so I've been told by a certain three-year-old.

SERENA: You are very good at hugs, that three-year-old is a smart kiddo. I'll text you when I'm done.

LEO: Okay, baby. I love you. You're an amazing, strong, independent woman. Promise me that you'll show him what he missed out on by walking away, but also hear him out.

SERENA: I promise. Now get back to your meeting, Officer Talbot. Or you'll get in trouble.

LEO: You ARE trouble.

SERENA: Whatcha gonna do, cuff me again? *winky face emoji*

LEO: Damnit woman, now I'm sporting a chub sitting across from the provincial commissioner. You're evil. *devil emoji*

SERENA: Love you... *heart eyes emoji*

That brief exchange with Leo was exactly what I needed to relax. But now that I'm waiting at a Starbucks in Westport for the man I used to call Dad, I'm freaking out again.

Even though he wanted to come to Dogwood Cove and see where I lived, I couldn't handle that. Not yet, at least.

My hands twist the paper cup full of steaming chamomile tea around and around on the table as my eyes continuously dart between the door every time it opens and my phone that's face up on the table.

I'm early. I thought it would help if I was here and settled, but it's done the opposite and given me too much time to feel awkward and weird.

"Serena?"

My head snaps up.

"Dad."

The chair makes a loud scraping noise as I push it back to stand. We hug. It's awkward, stilted, and forced, but my mind still registers the fact that he smells the same, like Old Spice soap. It's an aroma I haven't been able to handle smelling ever since he left. I even walked out on a first date the second we met because he smelled like Old Spice.

"Thank you for meeting me, honey."

With the initial shock of seeing him over, I register more details. He's thin — too thin — and his skin looks sunken somehow. This is not the vibrant man I remember. His voice sounds weak, but his grip on my hand is strong as we sit down.

"Do you want something to drink?"

He shakes his head. "No, I just want to look at you for a minute. Is that okay? You've grown into such a beautiful woman."

I cast my eyes down at the table. This is just as uncomfortable as I thought it would be, but not for the reasons I expected. There's a heaviness to my dad's demeanor. A weight that goes beyond guilt. Suddenly, I wish I had asked Leo to come with me.

"I'm not sure what your mother told you about why I left, but I assume you know the basics." He looks almost hopeful, as if he doesn't want to rehash everything, but too damn bad; I need answers.

"She told me you had a gambling problem and almost lost my money for ballet school," I say bluntly, staring him in the eyes. "But she didn't say why you disappeared from my life and never even reached out." I tug my hand free of his, bringing it to my cup of tea, steeling my heart against the pain etched on my father's face.

"That's... Yes. That's most of it. I'd like to tell you everything, if you'll listen."

I nod. Isn't that why I'm here, to finally get some closure on why he left?

"Right. It started when the company I was working for when you were just starting high school did some restructuring. Your mom and I didn't want to let you know, you were so young, but I ended up with double the workload and no extra time to do it. The stress spilled over and became unmanageable. I knew your mom was handling everything for you and ballet, so I started going to the casino after work to unwind. At first, it was just one or two poker games a week. Nothing major, just a way to leave the stress of work behind before I headed home to you and your mom. I would win quite often. Just enough to get me hooked on the thrill of it. But after a few months, well, I guess you could say it started to get out of control." He drags in a ragged breath, his hands twisting together. "I'm simplifying things, but let's just say I quickly fell into a habit of hitting the casino almost every night. Your mom thought I was working even longer hours, but I wasn't. Quite the opposite. I was neglecting work, dropping the ball on all kinds of things just so I could escape everything and play poker. I was good, too. I won more than I lost. That was the problem. The high of winning became my driving force. Even when your mother found out and told me to stop, I couldn't. I just got better at hiding it."

"Dad," I murmur when I see the shame etched all over his face. The pain and guilt he has been carrying is obvious, and makes my own pain pale in comparison.

He holds up one shaky hand. "Let me finish, sweetheart, please. I need you to know it all before you decide if you can forgive me. You were in grade eleven when I lost my job. Your mother and I told you it was cutbacks, and everything would be fine. After all, we had the money from your mom's parents for ballet school already set aside, plenty of savings, and of course I was confident I'd find another job. But I didn't. I told you that I did, but the truth was, I lied to your mother, and you, for almost a year or so. In reality, I was at the casino. I burned through our savings, racked up debt, but still, I couldn't stop. I'd win enough to pay things down, then lose it all the next month. I fooled myself into thinking I could handle it; if I could just win big once to get things stable for us financially, then I'd quit. But that day never came. It never does with gambling. When your mom found me about to withdraw money from your ballet school fund, she forced me to see what I was doing. I was destroying our family, and I was about to destroy your future."

His eyes are watery, and I'm sure mine are, too.

"You were the one thing that could get through my fog of addiction. I couldn't take away your dreams. When your mom handed me the brochure for a rehab facility in Alberta, I made plans to go as soon as possible. I stayed there for two months, signed the divorce papers your mom sent me, and promised her I would never *ever* try to take anything from you again."

He stops talking and slowly the sounds around us — the other patrons in the café, the noise of the espresso machine — it all filters back in.

"But why did you stay away?"

Such a simple question, and after everything he's shared, maybe I shouldn't ask. But I need to know.

"Because for years I was terrified I wasn't strong enough. Addiction is a lifelong sentence. A disease. My brain is forever changed from it. It might not have been drugs or alcohol, but it had much the same effect. I have to live every day of my life avoiding temptation, reminding myself why gambling is so dangerous for me. And I didn't know if I could withstand your rejection if I reached out and you wanted nothing to do with me."

"You're my father. And you left me."

"I know. And I've lived with that guilt, and an emptiness in my heart, ever since."

"So why now? Why did you finally reach out now?"

Dad shifts in his seat, reaching down to the bag I didn't even realize he had with him. He pulls out a folder, placing it on the table between us.

"I know I can never make up for leaving, and money is the most trivial way of trying to apologize. But I'm a dying man, Serena. This is all I have to give you." He slides the folder over to me, and I pull out some paperwork. My eyes skim the top that reads *Last Will and Testament of Gareth Matheson.*

"Daddy. What is this? What do you mean you're a dying man?" My eyes are filling rapidly.

"Liver cancer. Such a joke since I was never a drinker. My doctor estimates I'm down to weeks left."

He says the words so quietly, so clearly, yet it takes me forever to absorb them.

"Weeks."

"Yes. Oh Serena, I'm so sorry I didn't reach out sooner. I wanted to. But I was so scared. It was my sponsor through Gamblers Anonymous who told me not to put it off any longer if I wanted any time with you at all."

The tears spill over, streaming down my cheeks. I push back my chair and bolt out the door of the Starbucks. Somehow over the last hour it started to rain; one of those late summer storms where the air is humid and warm.

I let the droplets hit my face and mix with my tears. When I sense my dad come up behind me, I spin around, letting my fists hit his chest.

"Why didn't you find me sooner? Why now? Why did you wait so long?"

"Oh, honey." He folds me in for a hug and I go, sagging against his frail, weak body.

"It's not enough time, Daddy," I sob.

"It would never have been enough. And that's my fault, sweetheart. I'll never forgive myself for staying away so long, but I hope you can forgive me someday. And just believe that I did what I thought was best for you at the time. Any decisions I've made, I've always made based on my love for you."

And there, in the rain outside of a coffee shop, I feel the last weight on my heart lift. And I say the only three words that are needed right now.

"I forgive you."

Chapter Twenty-Four

Leo

Finally. 7pm on the dot. I hurry out the door of the police station and get into my truck. Kat is with Violet tonight, and I already told her I would be home late, if at all. Turns out, having balance and freedom as a dad is possible when I just allow my family to help the way they want.

I check my phone one last time. There's still no message from Serena since the one she sent earlier this afternoon. That one just said she was going to have dinner with her dad. I'm hoping that means things went well.

But just in case, I stopped by The Nutty Muffin on my break and had Mila put together a box of treats, all of Serena's favourites. And now I'm on my way to the studio to see her.

I need to see for myself that she's okay after talking to her dad.

But when I pull up to the studio, the lights are all off. She still isn't home.

My phone flips around in my hand as I debate back and forth whether to text her. I don't want to interrupt them, but I have to admit, I'm going a little crazy with worry.

When my phone starts to vibrate, I almost drop it in my hurry to open the message. But it's not from her. And neither are the ones that follow immediately after.

MAX: Hey buddy, any word from Serena?

SAWYER: Not that we're being nosy or anything.

MAX: Bro we totally are. We're channeling our inner teenage girls right now.

BECKETT: Speak for yourself. I'm content to leave Leo and Serena alone.

SAWYER: Fuck that. She's basically family. And we're allowed to be nosy about family.

BECKETT: Remind me again, how old are you?

SAWYER: Not as old as you.

MAX: He's five minutes older, Sawyer. Five. Minutes.

JUDE: I miss all the good shit. What's going on with Serena? Why are we being nosy fuckers?

SAWYER: Bro! Good game last night, but what the fuck was with that missed pass from Grayson?

JUDE: ... Last time I checked I was the professional athlete and you were rescuing kittens from trees. How bout you check that attitude.

SAWYER: Fuck off.

LEO: Hey guys, as much as I hate to interrupt whatever this is, I'm gonna mute your ass so I don't miss any messages from Serena.

MAX: Still no word, huh? I'm sure she's fine.

SAWYER: Yeah, if her dad does anything to upset her, he's gonna have all of us to answer to.

JUDE: Terrifying, Sawyer. Truly.

SAWYER: Shut up.

JUDE: You shut up.

BECKETT: Guys. Seriously? Leo, keep us posted if and when you can.

I hit the mute option on the group chat with my cousins just as headlights flash in my rearview mirror.

"Thank fuck."

I climb down from my truck and jog back to Serena's car, opening her door before she's even had a chance to kill the engine.

"Are you okay?" I ask, reaching my hand in to take hers as she steps out of her car. I've got an irrational need to toss her over my shoulder and carry her inside all caveman like, just so I can get her alone and hold her.

Because even if she doesn't need it, I do. I need to know my girl is alright.

"Have you been waiting here for me?"

I simply stare at her. "Of course I have. Where else would I be?"

Her smile is warm but tired. I wrap my arm around her shoulders and steer her toward the door. Once we're upstairs in her apartment and she's on the couch, I kiss the top of her head.

"Be right back."

Then I run downstairs, grab the box of treats, and run back up. She's still sitting where I left her, but her legs are drawn up and tucked underneath her. I study her carefully as I take off my duty belt, placing it by the door. She doesn't seem angry or upset, but there is a heaviness to her mood.

I set the box down on the coffee table before sitting down next to her and opening my arms. "Come here, Tippy."

It's only once her body is tucked up against mine, her arms wrapped around my waist, that I let go of the worry I've had all day.

"Do you want to talk about it?"

"Not yet, if that's okay. When do you have to be home for Violet?"

"Kat's with her. I can stay."

"Good." Her voice is muffled as she turns her face into my chest.

We sit like that for a few minutes. It's killing me not to ask what happened, but if silence is what she needs, then that's what she gets.

Eventually, her head lifts and she reaches for the bakery box. "How did you know I'd need some sugar?"

I just laugh. "Because I know you. Chocolate is your comfort food."

She lifts out a brownie, takes a bite, then holds it up for me to share. Back and forth we go until it's gone and she still hasn't said a word about her father. Standing up, she walks to the kitchen. I hear the fridge open, then she's back with a glass of milk. Offering it to me, I shake my head, and she drinks it down before returning the glass to the kitchen and then coming back to sit beside me.

"He's dying."

It takes a second for those words to register in my brain.

"Wow," is all I can mutter at first.

"Yeah. Liver cancer. He doesn't have a lot of time, which is why he wanted to see me. And get this. Once he quit gambling, he got a new job, and now he makes a ton of money. He has one hell of a life insurance policy, and he's leaving it all to me when he dies. Money. The thing that tore my family apart in the end is what he's using to try and fix things. Because that's meant to make up for him being gone all this time." Her voice wavers, and I pull her back into my chest. "The thing is, I forgave him. And I meant it. I understand now why he left and why he stayed away. But it still feels so unfair, like some cruel punishment that he's only back because he's dying. And the money, I don't want it; I want him. But then again, I do want it. Because it's the answer to all of my problems. Does that make me a terrible person? That I'm relieved he's giving me money, even if it's only because he's dying?"

"God, no. Not at all."

"I told him I didn't want the money. I refused to take a copy of the will. I just, I can't do that. I can't take his money as some bizarre apology."

"Baby," I start, thinking carefully about what to say. "I think it's more than an apology to him. It's the only way he has to start making up for the last twenty years. I'm not saying it's okay or that you have to accept the money. But as another man who has been trying to make up for lost time, I'm just saying, cut him — and yourself — some slack. Look at his offer as more of a door opening, a way back into a relationship with your father."

She sighs, and I feel her body sag against mine just a little bit more.

"It all just feels so surreal. He's been out of my life for so long, and I thought I was over that. But now, knowing he's back only to leave me again, but this time forever? It hurts so much."

I hold her, letting her cry into my shirt. Seeing my beautiful, strong girl, so vulnerable and in pain is killing me. Especially since there is absolutely nothing I can do to make it better. No words I can say, nothing, will take this pain away.

Eventually her tears slow and she lifts her head, rubbing at the wet spot she left behind.

"Sorry," she whispers.

"Don't be. What can I do? Do you want some tea?"

"Actually." She casts her eyes down at her hands. "I feel bad for asking, but I think I need to be alone for the night." She winces before glancing back up at me. "I'm sorry. I appreciate you being here, really."

As much as it kills me to do so, I stand up and walk over to where I put all my gear when we came inside. "Don't ever apologize for asking for what you need."

Serena follows me over to the door before hugging me tightly. "Thank you. You're amazing, Leo Talbot. I love you and I'm thankful for you. Now go home to your little girl and cuddle her close."

"You'll call me if you want me to come back, right? Or just come over to my house. I'll leave the back door unlocked." My hand grips the door handle. I don't want to leave her like this, even if it is what she wants.

"I promise I'll call you if I need to talk. But don't be disappointed if I don't, okay? It's nothing to do with you, or us, it's just me. Please understand."

I cup her face in my hands, my thumbs gently stroking her jawbone. "Tippy, I'll never deny you something you need or want. It's just hard for me to leave you when I know you're upset."

She kisses me briefly, her hands resting on my chest, holding onto my shirt. "I know. And I won't pretend I'm not sad about my father. But I really do just want some time alone to process everything, maybe have a good cry, and then get some sleep. I'll see you tomorrow, okay?"

In the end, the knowledge that yes, she will see me tomorrow, even if she doesn't realize exactly how early she'll be seeing me...is what gives me the strength to kiss my girl one more time and then leave.

Once I've said goodnight to Kat, I walk down the hall to Violet's room and peek in the door. She's fast asleep, her arms stretched up over her head, in her usual position. I walk in and crouch down beside her bed. Stroking the little hairs back from her face, I lean down and kiss her forehead.

"I love you, my sweet girl. And I promise to never let you doubt that."

I'm already outside the studio when my cousins pull up in Sawyer's truck and start unloading their tools. "Hey guys, thanks for doing this."

Sawyer slaps me on the back. "No worries, man, this is what family does. Besides, you said there would be muffins."

"I've got those!" A feminine voice makes us turn to see Mila, Paige, Summer, and a couple other women I don't know walking toward us from the direction of the bakery. "The guys are on their way with the glass for the window, too."

They come to a stop in front of us and Mila opens the lid of a large bakery box, revealing a dozen of her signature apple nut muffins.

"Dig in."

"Good morning, Leo. Is Serena still asleep? She did not send us an update on how her conversation with her father went, so I confess, we are all quite curious."

I lift a muffin in greeting. "Morning, Paige. Yeah, I think she's still sleeping. When I left her place last night around ten she was okay. But I'll let her give you the details."

"What's going on?"

We all turn around at Serena's confused and still sleepy voice. She's wearing her pajamas, and her eyes widen almost comically when she sees everyone standing around. They get impossibly larger when a horn honks, and Ethan pulls up in a large truck with carefully wrapped sheets of glass in the back.

"Leo, what the heck is all this?"

I go over to Serena and kiss her cheek. "This is our friends and family showing you that we love you, and we've got your back, always."

"Where should we start?" Max asks before nodding at Serena. "Hey, Serena, how are you?"

"Stunned? Confused? Overwhelmed? Take your pick." She lifts her shoulders and looks at me with a baffled expression.

"I would think it would be obvious by our attire and the tools present that we are here to make any necessary repairs to the studio." Paige pushes her glasses up her nose. "Oh dear, I did not anticipate that news making you weep."

"Shut up, Paige, these are tears of gratitude," Serena sniffs before throwing her arms around Paige, and then everyone else in turn. When she finally reaches me, she squeezes me so tightly it makes it hard to breathe. "You did this, didn't you? You didn't need to, you know."

"You said it would be hard to sell without the repairs done. I wanted to, at the very least, take care of this for you."

"But if I take my dad's money, I could pay a contractor to do all this," she murmurs, and I put one finger over her lips.

"Your dad's money doesn't matter right now. Everyone who loves you wanted to help; all you have to do is let them. It's a lesson I'm learning for myself, and maybe you need to as well."

"We can learn together." She giggles softly and I grin down at her.

"I'll do anything together with you, Tippy. Anything."

"Anything?" She arches one brow. "Oh, Leo. You have *no idea* what you just committed yourself to."

My brows draw together in confusion. "What?"

Serena's smile is wicked when she says four words that have the potential to make anyone shrivel up in fear.

"Fall. Festival. Dance. Recital."

Chapter Twenty-Five

Serena

"You do know I'm meant to be an authority figure in this town," Leo grumbles and I can't contain my giggle.

"Sure, but you also told me you would learn anything with me, and I do mean anything."

His long sigh comes out sounding a little pained, and I stifle another laugh. I've been doing a lot of that lately — laughing, that is. I did eventually accept my dad's money, and the dance studio is securely paid off and in my name. Dad and I have gone to a couple of counseling sessions together over in Westport, and we're working through our feelings. At the end of the day, I love my father, and I'm grateful for a little bit more time with him. That's worth more than my studio. That's priceless.

"Yeah, I guess I never realized that meant learning a dance I'd have to perform on stage in front of the entire town."

"You've got Violet with you and the other moms." I try to reason, but he's having none of it, judging by the glare on his face.

"Nice outfit, buddy," his cousin Sawyer says as he walks up to us in a Dogwood Cove Fire Department T-shirt and jeans. "You really make that pink shirt pop. But where's the tutu?"

"Shut up," grumbles Leo. "Why are you here, anyway? Shouldn't you be wrangling children climbing all over you at the fire truck?"

"What, and miss the show? No way. I told Cap I needed to take a break so I didn't miss my cousin's big debut."

"Do I really have to do this, Tippy?" Leo turns to me, his eyes pleading. "Are you sure Aunt Claire can't do it?"

"Aunt Claire did not learn the choreography because *somebody* promised his daughter that he would do it." The woman in question comes up, her hands on her hips. "You'll get on that stage Leo, and you'll smile and have a good time."

"You'll be fine. The only thing anybody will think is that it's so adorable watching a hot dad up on stage with his beautiful daughter," I say quietly, squeezing his hand.

"I don't care about anyone thinking I'm a hot dad, except you." He dips down and presses his lips to mine. "Besides, I'm not so sure Violet is gonna enjoy looking at videos of her father making a fool of himself when she's older."

I give him a gentle shove toward the stage where the rest of the girls and their mothers are waiting to go on. Violet is there with a little girl named Macy she's become friends with, while I've been arguing with Leo over the pink shirt all the performing parents are wearing. Okay, so it's a little snug on him, but that isn't a problem — at least not for me.

"You can do this. Stop being a big baby."

"You owe me for this one," he growls under his breath, flashing me a dark look.

I just wink back at him. "I'll make it up to you tonight, don't worry."

Leo reluctantly heads over to the stage, and I make my way to the area just in front where I'll be leading the girls, and their parents, in our dance for the fall festival.

Despite handling the coordination of the police department for the festival, Leo managed to get coverage for himself so he could spend the day with Violet and me. We woke up together at his house with a little girl nestled in between us after she made her way into our bed in the middle of the night. Any trepidation I had about Violet's acceptance of me as part of their family disappeared in that moment when she snuggled up to me in the dark.

Once we got to the festival, Violet was her usual shy self, except instead of clinging to Leo, she hung onto me. The knowing glances my friends gave me when they saw the three of us together had me preening a bit. I'm happy — so happy — and I don't care who knows it.

"This is adorable," Ashley swoons as she and the rest of my friends come up beside me.

"Yeah, but also, excellent blackmail evidence." Finn snaps a picture before I can slap his phone out of his hand.

"Finn, don't you dare scare him off. You guys need to make nice with Leo. Be friends with him."

"Don't worry, Serena, Leo's a good guy. He fits in with you, and with us, just fine," Ethan comments, wrapping his arms around Summer from behind. "I was surprised when he said he wanted to leave Violet at home for our wedding. You guys know she's welcome to come."

I shiver at the thought of the week in the Cayman Islands we have coming up to celebrate Ethan and Summer. They wanted something small and intimate, and that's exactly what it'll be. Just us friends at a beachfront resort on a small tropical island.

We each get our own private suite on the beach. Which is why little Miss Violet is staying home...

I can't wait.

But first, we need to get through this dance performance. I give my cue to the person at the side of the stage, and they press play on our music. As I start to lift my hands and move, my adorable class of girls follows along in that super cute way only toddlers do. The adults on stage are with them, swinging their hands and turning around, encouraging their little ones.

Then there's Leo.

He's concentrating so hard his brow is furrowed, but every now and then I see him steal a glance down at Violet and smile. It's enough to almost make me lose track of the steps.

When the music ends, there's a roar of applause and cheers, most of it coming from Leo's cousins.

"Daddy dance pwetty!" Violet announces when they get over to our group, earning a few discreet chuckles.

"Yes, he certainly did," I reply, reaching a hand out to run my hand over her blonde hair I tamed into a braid this morning. "And so did you, missy."

Violet beams. She loves dance, almost as much as I did at her age. That's why I set the extra money from my dad aside, after paying off the studio mortgage, of course, for dance school for Vi. If she wants it.

"Hey kiddo, want to come with Uncle Sawyer over to the firetruck?"

Violet frowns at Sawyer, and Leo just shakes his head. "I'll come too, baby girl."

"No, Rena come."

"Maybe after that, we can hit up the Scoops stand and get some ice cream?" Leo's Aunt Claire asks, and Vi nods vigorously. "And then we're going to check out the animals." She winks at Leo and I. "And give the grown-ups some time to themselves."

That time to ourselves doesn't happen after the firetruck or the ice cream. But I'm okay with it. Because Violet wanting to be with me? That's close to the best feeling in the world.

But it's not quite *the* best.

That honour is reserved for moments like this one. Sitting with Leo on the small Ferris wheel bench, letting it lift us up into the dusk-lit air.

Violet has gone home with Aunt Claire for a sleepover, so it's just the two of us for the rest of the night. Well, the two of us, plus all our friends scattered throughout the festival with plans to meet up later for the fireworks show.

"You know, from now on, I'm leaving all the dancing to you, Tippy." Leo leans over and kisses the side of my neck before dropping his hand down to my thigh. I'm starting to wonder if he had ulterior motives when he encouraged me to wear this long stretchy skirt today. I only agreed because it was an unseasonably warm day for early October. That and the skirt looks really good with my brown boots.

"Why? You did so well." I can't help but tease him. "And sparkly pink is definitely your colour."

"What was with that shirt, anyway? Did it have to be so shiny?"

"The girls picked it out." I shrug, leaning my body against his strong arm. His lips find my head, resting there as the ride takes us higher and higher. Eventually, his hand, lazily drawing circles on my leg, starts to move up.

"Leo," I whisper, shifting in the seat. "What are you doing?"

"Just enjoying the view."

I crane my head up at that innocent statement to see his eyes gazing at me like two bottomless green pools of love and desire.

His fingers are tracing the very tops of my thighs now, and my body is starting to burn with anticipation. "We can't... "

"Really? Why not?" His lips find my neck again, gently sucking, licking, teasing my skin. I stifle my moan.

"Because...I don't...I don't know." I gasp when he bites gently, then soothes the spot with his tongue.

"Then let go, Tippy. Trust me."

Those are the magic words.

My legs fall open, and Leo's hands move quickly to the elastic waistband of my skirt, sliding underneath. He strokes up and down the silky fabric of my panties.

"Fuck, you're wet, baby." He pushes them to the side and dips his fingers between my legs.

"God. Jesus, Leo."

How this man gets me from zero to a hundred in no time at all is one of my life's greatest mysteries. A delicious, toe-curling, heart-pounding mystery.

"You're going to come on my fingers on this Ferris wheel, and then when we get home tonight, you'll do it all over again. In *our* bed. In *our* house."

"Yes," I gasp as he plunges his fingers into me.

"You're everything to me, Serena Matheson. You get that now, right? Everything." His voice is a rich rumble in my ears, the sound adding to the sensory overload currently flooding my body.

"I love you. I love you. I love you," I chant, fighting desperately to keep my volume low enough so that everyone around us doesn't figure out what's going on.

But when Leo's fingers curl around and hit that magical spot inside of me that he can always find without error, I know I'm going to lose control. So I grab his face and smash our lips together, desperately riding out my release in our kiss. He swallows my moans, our tongues tangle, plunging in and out of each other.

He keeps on kissing me, and keeps on stroking me, until my body starts to shake. Slowly, he pulls out his hand, lifting his fingers to his mouth and sucking each one of them. "You're delicious, Tippy."

I bite the inside of my cheek to stop myself from begging him to figure out how to fuck me right then and there. Because he'd do it. I know that much is true — Leo would do *anything* for me.

"Do we really need to stay for the fireworks?"

His satisfied smile makes it seem as if he's the one who just had a spectacular orgasm, but I know that's not true. I can feel the evidence of that straining against his pants.

"You promised your friends we would."

"Friends, shmiends. I wanna go home and do *that* again."

"Baby, we have the rest of our lives for *that*, and I have to stay till the end of the fireworks anyway. Remember?"

I pout, but I don't mean it. "Fine, but we're getting apple cider."

Leo's laugh is warm and relaxed. And so familiar it makes my heart want to burst. I don't know how I got so lucky to have a second chance with this man, but I will forever be grateful.

The ride comes to an end and we climb off, sharing a secret smile about what happened at the top of the wheel.

"Why do you have orgasm face?"

I whirl around and point my finger at Mila. "You hush."

"Oh my God, you guys totally got busy on the Ferris wheel!" She nudges Jackson. "See? I *told* you all the action happens up there."

My face heats up, and I know I'm turning red. Thank goodness it's almost dark out. "Okay, let's just drop it and go find a spot for the fireworks."

I start to tug Leo in the direction of the best viewing spot for the fireworks, but he pulls me to the side and wraps his arms around my waist.

"I'm not embarrassed, baby, and you shouldn't be, either."

"I'm not," I protest, my hands coming up to rest on his chest. "I've never been embarrassed by my sexuality and I'm not about to be now. I just don't need my friends shouting it out where anyone can hear."

"I get it. I want to keep you and your orgasms all to myself, anyway."

I smirk up at him. "Possessive much?"

Leo drops a kiss onto my lips. "Maybe I am, so what? You've been mine for over twenty years, Serena. Even if we weren't together the whole time. I loved you then, and I love you now. And I promise I'll love you forever."

Epilogue

Leo

Serena's dad passed away about two months after they reunited. In those weeks leading up to his death, he stayed in Dogwood Cove so that the two of them could have as much time together as possible. Serena's mom came out for a week, and seeing the three of them talk and reach a point of peace and acceptance with everything was inspiring.

It also gave us time to throw together a wedding at city hall with Ethan officiating. Serena's dad was able to walk her down the aisle and join us for a small reception at Camille's café. As much as I wanted to give Serena her dream wedding, when she confessed the only thing important would be her dad attending, we knew what we had to do.

"Hey husband."

I'll never get tired of hearing that. "Hey wife," I say as I turn around to see Serena walking toward me, a platter full of burgers and chicken in her hands. I take it from her, stealing a kiss in the process. "You ready for chaos?"

"If by chaos you mean all of our friends, your cousins, and everyone's kids descending on us, then yes. I'm ready."

Two years ago, I moved back to Dogwood Cove with my daughter, fully believing I would be a single dad forever. I never counted on finding Serena here. But today we're celebrating our reunion with a barbecue. Everyone's coming: my aunt, uncle, and cousins, plus their significant others, and all of Serena's friends, plus their families. It's going to be loud and busy, and I can't wait. Violet has been running around all morning, asking every two minutes how much longer until everyone arrives. She's got some hero worship going with Reid and Abby's daughter Layla and loves to dote on Summer and Ethan's little guy Sloan.

"They're here!" Violet's shout echoes through the house, all the way to the backyard, and we both chuckle. To say she's overcome her shyness would be an understatement. Violet is a confident, kind, social butterfly of a girl who still loves to dance.

Not long after that, the yard is full of our loved ones. Beer and other drinks are handed out, kids are running around with popsicles, and Serena is in her element, laughing with all of her friends.

"Hey man, you ready for a rematch tomorrow?" I turn at the sound of Wyatt's voice. Paige's husband is a total adrenaline junkie, and the owner of an adventure tourism company in town. On the last weekly trail run the guys all do that I was able to join, he challenged me to a race on one of the local rock climbing routes. It was too close to call, so we've got a redo scheduled for this weekend.

"You know it. Are you ready to admit defeat? I maintain that my hand reached the top first."

"Gentlemen, gentlemen, we'll settle this on the rock." Finn drapes his arms around me and Wyatt's shoulders. Out of all the guys, he's the one I'm closest to for some reason. "Today, we eat and drink, and tomorrow we climb. Well, you climb. I don't."

Good-natured laughter follows. Finn has always taken our ribbing about his distaste for outdoor sports well, half the time he's the one who's making the jokes.

"How you ever reached the decision to move to a small town where outdoor recreation is such a big part of life, I will never understand," Ethan chimes in.

"Best decision of my life."

"Same here," Wyatt adds.

"I couldn't agree more," I say, lifting my bottle of beer. We all tap them together and take a drink.

"Daddy, is it time?"

At the exact same time, all five of us guys hush Violet with a quiet "shh." My eyes dart around and thankfully, Serena is on the other side of the yard, oblivious to what's going on.

"Almost, sweetheart. But you gotta stay quiet, remember? Rena doesn't know what we're doing."

"I know, Daddy." Violet nods solemnly. "I didn't even tell Layla."

"That's good because she can be a real chatterbox," Reid mutters cheerfully. He should know, it's his stepdaughter.

"Yup," Violet says, turning to Reid with wide eyes. "Last week she told me all about how she heard her mom makin' strange noises and sayin' your name in a super weird way in the middle of the night, but when she went to your room to see what was wrong, the door was locked, and when she knocked, you used a...a —" Violet cups her hands around her mouth "— a *grown-up* word."

Reid turns bright red as the rest of us fight desperately to hold back our laughter.

"Looks like Layla's not the only chatterbox," Jackson whispers loudly, causing another wave of smothered laughter.

Jesus. Time to change the subject. I crouch down in front of my daughter and take her hands. "Listen kiddo, we'll ask Rena our important question after we've all had dinner. Think you can wait that long?"

Vi ponders that for a minute in a way only a kid can. "Yeah, I think so. I'm pretty hungry. And I don't wanna ask her when I'm hungry in case my tummy rumbles."

"Exactly." I kiss the top of her head. "Why don't you go and play with the dogs some more, and I'll get all the food off the grill so we can eat."

"Okay, Daddy!"

She skips off, and I watch her go back to playing with Mila and Jackson's two dogs. Maybe we should get a dog. Kids need pets.

"You're gonna make Serena one happy lady." Ethan hands me a fresh beer.

"That's the plan," I reply, taking a drink. "Seems only fair since she makes us happy every day."

Are you desperate to know what that important question is?!

Download an exclusive bonus scene by visiting https://bit.ly/JuliaJarrett_TN_bonus

ACKNOWLEDGMENTS

I try really hard not to pick favourites with my books... But, if I have to? This is it. Thank you so much to everyone who helped me bring Serena and Leo to life.

As always, to my KKSB sisters - thank you for being my supporters, my encouragers, my sounding boards, my brainstorming partners. There's no way I could do this without you.

Chelle Sloan – the best author friend a girl could ask for. You're amazing and I can't begin to tell you how much I appreciate you.

Kelly Kay, Erica, and Chris – thank you for all of your advice and feedback, and editing prowess in making this story the best it could be.

Carolina – thank you for being the better half of my brain and putting up with my chaos week after week.

Theresa and Alex – my crazy adores your crazy, and I'm so grateful to call you two friends.

Mr. Jarrett and the minions – thank you for putting up with Mama's ridiculous work schedules, highs and lows, creative bursts and slumps. You keep me sane, and drive me nuts all at the same time and I love you forever and wherever.

And finally my incredible readers – You made this series soar to heights I couldn't have imagined. Thank you for your love and support along the way. New readers and old, you've shown me over and over again that this is exactly what I am meant to be doing. And I couldn't feel more lucky. Don't be sad that Dogwood Cove is complete, because I'm not. We have friends in these pages we can revisit at any time, and I promise you that they will all make an appearance at some point in the future. You don't want to miss out on those Donnelly brothers... Trust me

.

ALSO BY JULIA JARRETT

<u>Dogwood Cove</u>

Always and Forever

Rumours and Romance

Work and Play

Truth and Temptation

Then and Now

Passion and Promises – A Dogwood Cove Novella Collection

<u>The Donnellys of Dogwood Cove</u>

Dare To Kiss you

Hate To Want You

Pretend To Love You

Promise To Marry You

Dare To Marry You – A Donnellys of Dogwood Cove Holiday Novella

One Night To Win You

<u>Standalone</u>

Seductive Swimmer - A standalone novel set in the Cocky Hero
World, inspired by Vi Keeland and Penelope Ward's Cocky Bastard series

About Julia Jarrett

Julia Jarrett is a busy mother of two boys, a happy wife to her real-life book boyfriend and the owner of two rescue dogs, one from Guatemala and another one from Taiwan. She lives on the West Coast of Canada and when she isn't writing contemporary romance novels full of relatable heroines and swoon-worthy heroes, she's probably drinking tea (or wine) and reading.

For a complete listing of Julia Jarrett books please visit www.authorjuliajarrett.com/books

Follow Julia:
Instagram @juliajarrettauthor
Facebook Reader Group: Julia Jarrett's Nutty Muffins
TikTok @julia.jarrett.author